Preface

At the outbreak of World War Two the little Somerset town of Yeovil, in common with so many others, discovered that overnight it had become a massive army camp. To add to their problems, the townsfolk also found that they were expected to house and entertain an influx of thousands of hastily mobilised servicemen and women. Accommodation for so many soldiers was hard to find and given at such short notice that some cynics said it was impossible to meet the requirement. To overcome this and to meet the vast arrival of manpower that even compulsory billeting could not cope with, tents and marquees were hastily erected upon commandeered land. All this had a drastic effect on the sleepy little market town.

The nearby airfield at the Royal Naval Air Station at Yeovilton held the men and aircraft of the Fleet Air Arm. This establishment rapidly expanded from a peace time complement to a war footing, again with a significant increase in personnel. This was particularly true for those needed to work on the 417 acres that contained the grass airfield in the early days of the conflict. The quiet little pubs of Ilchester, such as The Bull and The Dolphin, suddenly found themselves doing a roaring trade, much to the delight of the landlords.

Within Yeovil itself the Westlands Aircraft Works became a prime target for the German air force. They made several attempts to wipe the factory off the face of the earth, but although they came close, they failed to stop aircraft production.

All in all, the little town's population virtually exploded. Everywhere you looked or went there was ample evidence of the war. Armoured Bren Gun Carriers raced around the streets of Yeovil, their tracks churning up the tarmac roads and scraping the side of an odd car or two. Most of the men were in uniform, and those who were not received some icy and strange looks from the womenfolk.

Evacuee's from London and other cities poured into the little town to be safe from the nightly bombings that the major cities were enduring. The strange mixture of foreign languages of soldiers who had escaped from overrun countries, such as the Holland and

France, became commonplace. Later, the Americans arrived to add to the complex mix of the wartime town.

I have written these twenty short stories as a tribute to the men, women and children of the time who were unfortunate enough to have experienced the awful disaster of total war. The events I talk about mostly happened, and where possible I have used the names of the people involved. If I have, you will find them recorded in the index to this book.

The locations I have used in the area were in existence then, and some remnants, such as Houndstone Camp in Yeovil, are still there. As with any story that interweaves fact and fiction, some of the characters did not exist, nor indeed did some of the imagined events. That is not to say that these events could not have occurred, for logic dictates that they may well have. Some of the characters have been given an identity or description that may not actually have been theirs; in the interest of the story I have had to make these changes.

As usual, my thanks go to Sue Rickerby for translating my Somerset into a plainer language, and for John Hawkins for the photograph of where he once used to live, the Pen Mill Cottages, where, in one of the stories, 'Browncie' dwelt.

Contents

Evacuees - 1st September, 1939. 4

Blimey! It Really Is War! - 13th September, 1939 11

For King and Country – Not Blooming Likely! - Late September, 1939 18

You Just Got to Eat - January, 1940. 25

A Jug of Cider - 1st June, 1940. 30

The Dance - 2nd July, 1940. 38

The Balloon Goes Up - 7th October, 1940. 43

Lufton Camp - 14th October, 1940. 58

U.X.B. - 6th November, 1940. 66

You'm Different- May, 1942. 73

Wasted Bread - July, 1942 78

Cider and Bombs - 5th August, 1942 86

The Burning Bomber - 23rd January, 1943. 96

The Price of Oil - 1st September, 1943. 103

The Lost Love- 30th March, 1944 115

Secret Army - 4th June, 1944. 124

Royal Observer Corps- June, 1944. 130

Camp 405 - August, 1944. 137

It's Nearly Over Now - 18th April, 1945. 142

Back from the War - 3rd October, 1945. 147

Evacuees - 1st September, 1939.

The dirty black train expelled a large cloud of steam that for a moment or two obscured the engine as it squealed to an uncertain halt. A palpable feeling of wetness hung in the air and a little pool of water dripped slowly on to the four foot eight and a half inches of railway gauge that glistened beneath the train. Its source was a loose rubber hose that clung precariously to the frame of the steel monster and lay just beneath its huge coal bunker. To add to this scene of controlled chaos, the hissing train gave a sudden blast with its whistle, blowing a long and mournful sound that reminded one of a funeral dirge.

The train driver jumped down on to the platform and passed a sealed envelope to a waiting lady who quickly took it from him and ran awkwardly down the platform, the precious list of children's names held protectively close to her ample bosom.

Mrs Bowering stood fidgeting on the platform alongside at least forty other women, all anxiously awaiting their new responsibilities. They were there to collect the latest trainload of evacuees that had just arrived at the Yeovil Town Station from London. It should not have arrived at Yeovil at all, but no-one knew where it was supposed to have gone and the women, whose turn should have been the next day, were hurriedly called forward to collect their charges. The whole thing was an utter shamble, and, being typically British, those in authority muddled through it with the traditional "Stiff Upper Lip".

A uniformed station master strode purposefully along the platform, unlocking and opening the doors to each carriage as he did so. "Come along children," he encouraged as he did so. "You be yer!"

Women with hand made red-cross bands on their right arms hurriedly placed themselves at the open compartments. They cooed soothingly into the carriages with soft and gentle voices, and very soon frightened and scared little children alighted on to the long, crowded platform. There were no adults with them. The school teachers that had accompanied them had been unexpectedly

4

ordered off the train at Salisbury and told to return to London to collect even more children.

The carriage doors had then been locked to prevent the bewildered children from getting out. Each carriage had the eldest child appointed as the guardian for the rest of them and had been put in charge of two old army field canteens that contained the only drinking water the children would have until they reached Yeovil. Some of the carriages smelt a little, for some of the younger children were unable to control their bodily functions in the three-hour journey they had undertaken since leaving Salisbury Station.

Mrs Bowering put her hand to her mouth and she silently shed a tear at the sight of so many poor little waifs. Around their necks each had a loosely tied piece of string that led down to the little cardboard box that contained an obligatory gas mask. Some had small suitcases, others carried bundles of various sizes that were wrapped in newspaper or brown paper and to which they fiercely clung, their last tangible part of home.

Each child had an identification label firmly affixed to some part of their clothing, and that label bore a number and a name. Some children firmly held hands and would not let go of each other. What they all had in common was the whiteness of their faces and a look of fear and uncertainty etched upon them. One or two of them were crying, but most were deathly quiet. They had started out the trip with a sense of adventure, gaily singing 'The Lambeth Walk' and 'It's a Long Way to Tipperary'. All that had changed at Salisbury and with the loss of their familiar teachers the carriages had fallen strangely silent. Now they didn't know just what to expect.

Each red-cross lady ushered her newly found charges towards a large desk where a harassed looking woman with two helpers were sitting, quickly studying the newly arrived list and jotting down notes. This was the second train today that had arrived at the station and the lady in charge, Mrs Trump, had been told that yet another unexpected evacuee's train had been diverted to Yeovil and would arrive in the next few hours. Apparently, the train line between Crewkerne and Exeter had been bombed and no-one knew when it would be re-opened. In that case, she would now have more children to deal with than she had vacancies for, but she would do her best.

Each of the ladies at the desk now had a board in front of them with a list of names and numbers. The first official would call out the name of one of ladies waiting to receive her new charges. Then the lady on the right would call out the numbers of the children that would be allocated to each waiting woman. Finally, Mrs Trump would announce with some certainty the name of the children that the new "mum" was to receive.

The waiting women were being called forward in alphabetical order and it did not take long for Mrs Bowering's name to be announced. She made her way to the desk. The lady in the middle of the desk looked up and smiled. "Are you Mrs Bowering?"

"Yes, that be I!"

"You are down to take four children. Do you have any problem with that?"

Mrs Bowering shook her head. "Of course not, me dear! It baint a problem."

"Lovely!" The lady in the middle nodded to the helper on her right.

The woman scanned the list. "Numbers 14, 15, 16 and 17," she said.

The red-cross workers looked at the numbers pinned to their charges and ushered the children forward who matched the numbers called. As the lady reached for number 17, a little fair headed boy, a girl with number 18 on her label suddenly threw her arms protectively around him. "Leave me little bruvver be!" she shouted. "Mum said I gotta look after 'im!" The little boy burst into tears and grabbed his sister in a tight embrace. He screamed in terror as two red-cross ladies endeavoured to force them apart. The little girl kicked out at her aggressors, giving one of the ladies a painful kick on the shin. "Leave us be! Leave us be!" she screamed.

"Oh, my God!" cried Mrs Bowering. "You can't split up a brother and sister like that! Here, I'll take him as well!"

The lady in the middle quickly reminded her, "We've only got you down to take four, you know."

Mrs Bowering nodded. "Yes, I know that. Give me number 18 as well. One of the other single children can be re-allocated to another lady."

Mrs Trump, the lady in the middle, shook her head. "It's not as simple as that. They have already been allocated and they can't be changed."

"Well bugger me! Who bloody well says so?" challenged Mrs Bowering.

Mrs Trump stood up. "I do! I'm in charge here!" she shouted. "There are more children on the way that we are not expecting, and finding them somewhere to stay is going to be hard enough as it is. The numbering stays the same. You get whom I choose to give you." She spoke with a trembling voice that indicated the tremendous pressure she was under.

"How can you be so bloody heartless to split up a brother and sister?" snapped Mrs Bowering. "I've got room on the farm for another. Us'll manage somehow."

"Don't be so bloody stubborn! Let her take the extra child!" another lady called supportively from the crowd.

The little girl looked through wet blue eyes pleadingly towards Mrs Trump. "Please Miss," she said, sniffing back tears. "Let me stay with me little bruvver! I promise we won't be any trouble."

Mrs Trump sighed loudly, for she knew she was beaten. Taking her pencil, she altered the lists. "So be it then, Mrs Bowering. You shall have your way. I shall allocate you five children."

One of the waiting ladies called out an ironic "Hoo-bloody-ray!" and several others clapped their hands, for they could all see the injustice of what could have happened.

Mrs Trump sat down and consulted her list once again. "Mrs Bowering, you have the following children now assigned to your care." She pointed at the children. "Number 14, William Butcher, aged 5. Number 15, Shelby Overington, aged 5. Number 16, Jane O'Rourke, aged 6. Number 17, Alexander Delahaye, aged 5." She stopped for a moment as she adjusted something on her list. "And number 18, Jessica Delahaye, aged 6."

As she spoke each child was led forward in turn, a ration book bearing each waif's name being passed over to Mrs Bowering. They gathered around her, little Jessica still grasping her brother firmly. "Thank you, Miss," she said, still sniffing back tears. "Me mum would have bloody well killed me if I'd lost him!"

Mrs Bowering glowed, for she liked the way that this little fair haired girl protected her brother, but she reflected that she might have to teach her some more pleasant language. She led her new charges away for a little distance, and, kneeling, calmly spoke to them all. "Listen children," she explained in a soothing voice. "I know that you are all very frightened and scared, but there is no need to be. Your mums and dads all love you very, very much, but the nasty Germans are coming to bomb your towns so they want you to be somewhere safe until all this is over. Then you can go home, when the war is over."

Number 16 spoke in a hopeful tone. "Will that be next week, Miss?"

Mrs Bowering sadly shook her head. She chose her words carefully before she spoke. "No Jane, I am sorry to say that it will not be. It may take some time." The little girl's eyes became downcast. With a bright smile on her face, Mrs Bowering said, "Treat this like a holiday. You must call me Aunty Vera while you are staying with us out on the farm. Come along children, follow me."

Aunty Vera led the way out of the station and walked towards a car that was parked at an odd angle in the road. The driver's door opened and a ruddy faced farmer got out. He looked towards his wife with a questioning look on his face. "I thought you said we 'ad to 'ave four of them me dear?"

She smiled brightly. "Did I darling? Then I must have been mistaken."

The farmer nodded, for 43 years of happy marriage to the same woman had taught him to accept what his wife had said. He smiled as he lifted the boot of his car and took whatever luggage the children had. Mrs Bowering opened the back door of the car and ushered them in. The couple then slid into the car and with a practiced ease slammed their doors shut. Mr Bowering turned around in the front seat and gave the children a huge grin. "Hello, kids!" he said brightly. "Call me Uncle Jack! Who's hungry then?"

The children looked shyly at each other whilst the elderly couple exchanged knowing glances. Jessica looked uncertainly around her. "Me brother and me is!" she stated firmly. With a huge grin on his face, Mr Bowering reached into his pocket and pulled out a rosy red apple. He passed it to Jessica who said in a suspicious voice, "What's this?"

He frowned. "Why God Bless you child, 'tis an apple of course!"

"An apple? What's that?"

Mr Bowering shook his head in bewilderment and looked at his wife with an astonished look on his face. "You mean to tell me that you've never had an apple before?" he asked in an incredulous voice. Jessica shook her head. "You eat them my dear," he grinned. "You just bite into it and see!"

The little girl held the apple before her face and sniffed it. Cautiously she bit into it and suddenly her face lit up in a beaming smile. Quickly she took another bite and handed it to her brother. "Here Alex," she urged. "Quick, take a bite before they want it back!"

Mrs Bowering chuckled brightly. "Bless you my child, we won't take it back. That whole apple is just for you." She looked at her husband with a stern gaze and ordered, "Jack!"

The farmer smiled.

"Alright, my love," he said. The farmer, a beaming smile upon his face, took out an apple for each of them from his voluminous pockets and passed them across to the children. The look of pure delight on their faces as they tasted the fruit for the first time was a picture to behold.

"You know something, Vera," he whispered across to his wife.

"What?"

"I think that I'm going to enjoy having these kids on the farm!"

Historical note: At 11.07 a.m on Thursday the 31st August 1939 the order that was to tear families apart was urgently transmitted throughout the British Islands, 'Evacuate forthwith!' Operation Pied Piper was rapidly put into place and during the first four days of September nearly 3 million people were transported away from the towns and cities to a place of safety in the countryside.

Blimey! It Really Is War! - 13th September, 1939.

On the 3ʳᵈ September 1939, the war against Germany was officially declared by the then Prime Minister, Mr Neville Chamberlain. There was a surreal feeling amongst the civil population in Yeovil because apart from the nearby Air Station putting up additional fighter aircraft flights over the town, nothing really seemed to have changed that much. All that complacency began to change on the 10ᵗʰ September 1939 when the Advance Party of the 1ˢᵗ Battalion Coldstream Guards arrived in Yeovil and were billeted in houses in and around the small country town, much to the dismay of some of the original occupants.

The woman was listening to a harassed looking man, her arms folded firmly across her chest in an open act of defiance. "I'm sorry Mrs. Cheney, but you have no option but to accept the billeting of four soldiers in your house," explained the grim-faced council official in a tired tone. "They will be arriving tomorrow, probably sometime in the afternoon. Please have their room ready for use by then."

"But.........."

The council official who oversaw billeting soldiers in the Pen Mill area of Yeovil held up his hand in a stopping motion. "No buts, Mrs Cheney. Failure to comply with this order will result in imprisonment. There is a war on, you know!" His last part of the sentence was spoken with a veiled hint of annoyance in his voice.

Mrs Cheney sighed and shrugged her shoulders in defeat. She knew when she was beaten. "Alright Mr Fife," she said. "Four men it is. I only have one spare room and it only has a single bed in it. Where are they all going to sleep?

"Don't you fret yourself about that, Mrs Cheney," he said. "Each man will bring his own field blanket. A lorry will come around with some camp beds tomorrow at some time, one each for the other three men. They can all share the same room. The men will have their ration books with them so that you can get food for them."

"And who's going to pay for it?" she demanded in an indignant tone. "I'm a widow woman. I can't afford to keep them."

"Don't you worry about that either, Mrs Cheney." By now the council officer had a note of exasperation in his voice as he patiently explained, "An officer will come around here tomorrow and he will give you an advance of money for their keep. They are only expected to be here for a short while."

She spoke sharply. "Well! They had better do as I tell 'em, that's all I can say."

Mr Fife checked his list once again. "Right then! Thank you, Mrs Cheney. I'll be off now as I have a lot more billeting to do."

The widow Cheney forced herself to say, "Thank you, Mr Fife," and slammed the door shut with a bang to her two up and two down thatched cottage.

She grumbled softly to herself and then went determinedly upstairs and into to the spare room. She had already made up her mind that she would remove items of any value. At least the soldiers wouldn't be able to steal anything without her knowing about it. "Goodness me!" she said aloud. "This can't really be happening to me!" She hated the thought of having to let strangers stay in her house, and particularly four rough soldiers at that. "Still," she thought, offering herself some sort of consolation to the inevitable. "It will be nice to have some men-folk around the place again. It'll be some company for me."

She had been a widow since her husband, Tom, was killed during the First World War in 1917, fighting with the Somerset Light Infantry in France. She didn't even know where he was buried. Mrs. Cheney gave a slight shudder and then smiled to herself, for since that time she had always been alone, except for her two cats.

Two weeks later the soldiers ate their final breakfast in a stony silence, for today they were leaving. Although they had only been in the house for a short time they had been immediately made to feel at home. Mrs. Cheney had treated them as if they were her own children. The soldiers were very sad to be going, for they had to come to look upon Mrs Cheney as sons would a mother.

She clenched a crumpled white handkerchief to her moist eyes as she sniffed, "I'm going to miss you boys. You all take care now!

Tom got up and walked around the breakfast table. He put an affectionate arm around the woman they all called "mum" and gently squeezed her shoulders. "There, there, mother. Don't you fret about us! We're only off to another camp at Frampton, and that's not too far away. It's only in Dorset, and if we get any leave we will try and get a bus to Yeovil and come over here to see you," he promised. The others nodded their heads, indicating that they would too.

Tom, the eldest of the group and a Lance Corporal, turned to the others. "Come on lads. It's time for us to be going." Mrs Cheney stood up and Tom kissed her gently on the forehead. The others went around to her and each one gave her a little cuddle. The men, led by Tom, went to the door and picked up everything they had, although there was not much of it. They were still at peace time scales of equipment despite the manpower having gone up to war time entitlement. Because of this, Tom was the only one with a weapon, a short barreled .303 Lee Enfield rifle that had seen better days.

The men walked out of the house and turned to wave goodbye to Mrs Cheney. She held a handkerchief to her eyes and sorrowfully bid her "boys" a fond farewell. Quickly she shut the door as they went out of sight, and running up the stairs threw herself on to the bed, sobbing her heart out.

The four soldiers hurried along Sherborne Road before following the long road known as Park Street and they made good time. They stopped for a momentary breather at the bottom of Hendford Hill and snatched the chance for a quick Woodbine cigarette. When they had finished their smoke break, they started making their way up the steep hill to the rendezvous point, which was to be located outside the Quick Silver public house.

They were stopped at a miniature barricade halfway up the hill by two pompous special policemen who demanded to see their ID Cards before letting them through. When they reached the top of the hill they found that other men from their battalion were already assembling. Tom bade his section to sit down on the grass whilst he

13

went inside and reported them in to the Battalion Regimental Sergeant Major.

Mr. Petheridge, a large and imposing man, sat inside the public house behind a table, a glass of cold cider in front of him. Tom placed himself in a small queue behind some others and licked his lips in anticipation of the cold drink, for already it was a hot day. On the table the R.S.M. had a nominal roll in front of him and as the men reported themselves and their charges in, so he ticked off their names.

At 10 o'clock the officers of the battalion began to arrive, with the colonel of the regiment making a splendid entrance on a black horse loaned to him for the 16-mile march to their new location at Frampton in Dorset. It was here that they were to take over and extend the defensive trench system that had already been partly dug.

At 10.30 a.m. prompt, not a minute sooner or a minute later, the battalion R.S.M. came out of the Quick Silver inn, his lance corporal orderly marching obediently behind him. He took up his position on the main A37 road and steadied himself. "Battalion!" he roared. "Battalion, fall in!" The battalion bugler put his instrument to his lips and sounded the "Fall In."

Men quickly jumped to their feet and automatically fell in by their respective companies. There was much stamping and shuffling of feet as each man got himself into his allotted position. Two police motorcyclists kicked their machines into life, and, carefully threading their way along the road, they went on ahead. They would stop any traffic coming down towards the marching soldiers so that the 700 or so men could safely get past them. Tom pitied any driver coming up behind the battalion, for they would have a long wait before they could get by.

"Battalion! Battalion, right turn!" shouted the R.S.M. at the top of his voice. The soldiers lifted their knees and spun around to the right as one, stamping their feet hard on the ground. The R.S.M. smiled to himself, for the Coldstream Guards prided themselves on their drill. The colonel trotted along the column of troops like the red-coated leader of a hunt, his men the pack of hounds. His huge black horse snorted and tossed its head as he did so, eager to break into a trot or gallop.

"Not too far to go men," he called brightly as he rode along the line of soldiers. His men were fallen in three deep and split up into troops. Each troop was led by a subaltern whilst a major would lead in front of his three troops as the Company Commander.

Four companies of men standing at attention waited patiently for the order to move. The colonel reached the head of the column where his unit headquarters officers awaited him. "Nice day for a stroll, gentlemen!" he called affably.

"Just the ticket to work up an appetite for lunch sir!" one of them called back.

The colonel laughed. "Start them off, adjutant!" he ordered.

The adjutant saluted. "Very good, sir!" he replied. He turned towards the lead troop of men and shouted in a voice, which was about half as loud as the R.S.M.'s, "The battalion will advance in easy order. Battalion – advance!"

The colonel led off, his horse at a walking pace. The men of the company headquarters started first, following their officers. As each troop marched off, the following troop was set off by their commanders.   Within five minutes the 1st Battalion of the Coldstream Guards were marching easily down the main A37 road towards Dorchester. Those who had arms carried them at the trail.

A lone Bloom and Voss prototype BV141 aircraft had flown inland from its home base in the friendly country of Spain and across the Bay of Biscay, nearing the extremities of its range of 1900 kilometres. It had been stripped of its bombs and only carried a third of its ammunition to lessen its weight. Carrying extra fuel in lieu, it had been ordered to make a surprise photo-reconnaissance of the Westland Aircraft Works and airfield.

It was an odd looking flying machine because it only had one BMW 801A-O engine straight in line with the fuselage, and that was where you would normally expect to find the cockpit. The cockpit pod itself was off centre and to the right of the main fuselage, giving the impression of a large Perspex bubble on top of the wing.

Fritz Lutz, the pilot, was flying low to avoid detection and a mere 100 feet above the road, occasionally rising a little higher to miss any particularly large tree.

His observer yelled excitedly and pointed towards the approaching battalion. The column of soldiers could quite clearly be seen on the road. "Herr Kapitan! Infantry!"

Hauptmann Lutz spotted the column of men and spoke hurriedly into the intercom to his remaining member of crew, the rear gunner. "Do not open fire Hans! I repeat; **do not open fire**!" The captain emphasised the word *NOT*, for this part of the war was labelled "the phoney war" and Hitler secretly hoped that he could persuade Britain to either stay out of the war or to join him.

The throaty roar of an approaching aircraft took the battalion completely by surprise. The aircraft was so low that its black German crosses could be clearly seen displayed on its wings. Although the captain of the aircraft had orders not to open fire, unless fired upon, he had other intentions on his mind. Seeing a man leading the battalion on a beautiful black horse, he deliberately dropped his aircraft down to 50 feet. The horse reared up in panic and bolted back down the way it had come as the screaming aircraft passed overhead, its propeller wash almost blowing men over.

On the ground officers frantically blew their whistles, urging their men to take cover. They could not open fire on the approaching enemy, for they had no ammunition for their weapons. It was yet to be issued despite the unit being at war. For all of them who had not experienced the First World War it was their first real taste of the enemy.

Men dived off the road, taking shelter wherever they could. At any moment, the old seasoned soldiers expected the rat-a-tat-tat of the aircraft's machine gun, but fortunately it never came. Within a few seconds the aircraft was over and past, roaring towards its target.

Fritz Lutz and his observer laughed aloud as his rear gunner reported the mayhem that the pilot had caused. "It's a pity we won't be coming back this way," he called over the intercom. He heard his rear gunner join in the laughter.

The officers of the battalion were the first ones to recover, blowing their whistles to get men back on to the road and into some sort of semblance of order. Of the black horse, there was no sign. The colonel had been thrown from it, and, ruefully rubbing his bruised rump, he returned to the head of the column. His silent batman, looking a bit dishevelled and white, handed him a twisted walking stick. It looked like the colonel was going to have to walk to Frampton after all.

Tom made sure that his three men were alright and got them back into position on the road. "Bloody hell, corps!" said one of his men in an incredulous voice. "Them was bloody well Germans!"

"Aye," replied Tom. "He was flying a bit low and I swear I could see the bugger grinning in his cockpit!"

"Why didn't he open fire on us?" asked a nearby soldier.

Tom shook his head. "Might be like us – no ammunition," he explained.

Close by and in a vehement tone another soldier ruefully observed, "Blimey! It really is war!"

"You can say that again," replied Tom. "It looks as if we are really going to have to fight now."

For King and Country – Not Blooming Likely! - Late September, 1939.

John Brack perched precariously upon a small and empty five-gallon cider keg that, every now and then, wobbled furiously in Farmer Jones' barn. The building nestled snugly just beyond the sharp right hand bend about half way down Primrose Lane that led towards the tiny village of Mudford.

The young man slowly savoured his pint of cold dry cider and never felt better for being so unwell. His ruddy complexion was already being made redder by the strong, cloudy drink he was imbibing. The large grey, thick and uneven flagstones that made up the floor of the old barn added majesty to its high slate roof, for together they kept the air flowing coolly around the huge cider barrels. The barrels stood, as if on parade, like a row of Grenadier Guardsmen and were placed proud against the walls of the barn, five to each side and with an ordered distance between them. Brack had developed a ritual and he came here every Saturday to buy his weekly two gallons of cheap farmhouse cider.

He had been one of the first men called up for army service in 1939 and on the previous September day he had duly reported to the Medical Centre in Exeter where he had been closely examined by a military doctor. Brack had felt fine and so he was a little surprised when the young doctor who was examining him took longer than usual in listening to his fully expanded 30-inch chest.

The medical man had made a serious frown and left the room, only to return a few minutes later in the company of a very senior doctor. The older man listened intently through his stethoscope, ordering Brack to inhale and exhale alternatively. This he did so.

"When was the last time you saw a doctor?" he asked in a sympathetic tone.

Brack frowned. "I aven't," he explained. "I can't afford to get sick."

"Well, you should, young man. I am afraid we are going to have to reject you for any military service. You have an enlarged heart."

Brack was alarmed. "An enlarged heart? What be that?"

"It means that for a 21-year-old your heart muscle is bigger than it should be."

"Be I going to die!" he replied, a note of rising alarm detectable in his reedy voice.

"No, don't be too worried. It shouldn't affect you too much as a civilian, but I am afraid that you will never be allowed to join any of the armed forces. The rigorous military training that you would be expected to undergo would most certainly cause you severe medical problems. I will give you a certificate that exempts you from any future military service. Get yourself dressed and wait outside for the nurse to come and find you."

So Brack had failed his medical to enter the military, albeit through no fault of his own. He had his medical exemption certificate and that was that. He sat sipping his cold cider, secure in the knowledge that no-one could fault or blame him for not being in any of the armed forces. Not now, not ever. He forgot himself and gave a huge grin. Farmer Jones eyed him suspiciously over the top of his stone quart pot.

"You'm looks like thee be getting the cats cream, young'un. What be up?"

"Do I?" he replied, his voice a little disheartened. He then brightened up as he explained, "Shouldn't be, I suppose. Got my call up papers last week and went down for my medical all the way to Exeter yesterday. Never been that far before in me whole life! Come to think of it, afore yesterday I had never even been on a train!"

Jones nodded. "When do you expect to join?"

"I don't."

Jones looked surprised. "What do 'ee mean, you'm don't? Every single man your age is being called up. Why, even my own two boys is 'aving to go to Bristol next week for their medicals. I don't know how I be going to manage the farm without "em."

"Failed my medical," he explained.

"Failed thee medical? Why, you'm look as fit as a butcher's dog!" he said.

"Aye; and the strange thing be is that I feel quite well too. Doctors said I have an enlarged heart or something and so I baint fit for the military. Even gave me a piece of paper to say so." Brack pulled out his medical certificate and passed it over to Farmer Jones. Jones looked at it and re-read it a couple of times, an unbelieving look etched on his nut-brown face. This was suddenly replaced by a calculating expression.

"Do thee want to make thyself some easy cash me boy?" he asked.

Brack gave a start. "Easy money? I be always up for that."

"How would you like to make twenty quid then? No questions asked."

"Twenty quid?"

"Aye. Twenty quid."

Brack frowned. Twenty pounds was a lot of money to him, considering he only earned a pound a week in the gloving factory. That represented to him at least five months' wages. "Who do I have to kill for that?" he asked, a suspicious grin crossing his face.

"Thee doesn't 'ave to kill anyone, my boy. All you must do is stand in for my son, Freddie, when he has his medical. You jus' 'ave to be pretend to be 'e, like. Just answer up for him in the medical."

Brack shook his head. "They'd catch me out and put me in prison," he said.

Farmer Jones vigorously shook his head. "No, no, they wouldn't," he said enthusiastically. "How be they going to know who you be? My other son, Tony, wants to go and he'd swear blind he was your brother, if anyone asked."

"You want me to pretend to be Fred, is that it?"

Farmer Jones slapped Brack on his back. "You'm got it, me boy. You jus' complain a bit about your chest and you feel a bit dizzy sometimes. They'll soon find out about your dodgy ticker. Then they'll give you a certificate in Fred's name to say he is exempt from military service."

"Oh, I don't know about that!"

A crafty look came upon the farmer's face. "Who's going to know?" he asked. "There be thousands of young men going in for their medicals every day now. No-one will ever find out."

Brack scratched his head. "Twenty quid, you reckon?"

Farmer Jones nodded, his eyes bright with hope. "Yus! Twenty quid! You just give me the medical certificate exempting Fred and I give you the twenty quid, as easy as that."

"In cash?"

"In cash."

Brack thought for a while, or at least for twenty seconds. "O.K. I'll do it.

The frosty looking nurse looked at the list of names in her hands. "Frederick Jones?" she enquired. Tony Jones nudged Brack in the side and said in an exaggerated and loud voice, "They be calling you, brother, it must be your turn!" Jones sniggered behind a large and calloused hand that he suddenly drew across his face to mask his grin. Brack shook his fist at his "brother" and followed the nurse's directions.

He entered a room with about twenty other young men and quickly stripped down to stand naked alongside them. A tired looking doctor came along the row of men, eyeing each one up and down, searching for any obvious physical deformities. When he had completed that, he walked around behind them. He placed his stethoscope meticulously between each man's shoulder blades and in a bored tone asked each one to first inhale and then exhale. In a short while he was standing behind Brack.

"Inhale man," he ordered.

Brack inhaled and gave a cough. The doctor paused and replaced the stethoscope between his shoulder blades. "Cough again," he said. Brack coughed loudly, clearing his throat at the same time. "H-m-m," said the doctor, an interested frown playing across his once bored features.

"What's up doctor, baint my large heart playing up again be it?"

"What do you mean by that?"

Brack put on a little whining voice. "Me own doctor says I've got an enlarged heart or something. I don't know exactly what he means."

The doctor tut-tutted and pushed him out of the line. He turned to one of the two medical orderlies that were dutifully accompanying him. "Make out an exemption certificate for this man, Adams," he said. "Mark it as unfit for military service due to a large heart."

The orderly nodded. He prepared to write on the form, the millboard holding the piece of paper at the statutory 45 degrees. "Name?"

"Jones, Frederick Jones," Brack replied, an unseen smile playing triumphantly across his face.

Brack sat in the cider barn with the farmer, a free jug of well sampled cider beside him. "Well?" said Farmer Jones. Brack smiled and slowly pulled out a piece of paper.

"The medical exemption paper," he explained. Jones suddenly reached to snatch the proffered certificate away.

Brack hastily withdrew the offered paper. "Baint we forgetting something?" The young man felt a huge surge of power pass within him.

Jones nodded his head in understanding and reached inside his jacket pocket, taking out a large leather wallet. He counted out twenty separate pound notes and placed them on the upturned cider barrel that they were using for a table, pushing them towards his cohort in crime. Brack grinned, passing the medical certificate across to the eager farmer. He had never seen such money before, not all at once. Hastily he picked it up and, folding the notes, placed them in his pocket.

Farmer Jones smiled knowingly. "I know someone else who needs a certificate," he said, gently tapping the side of his nose with his index finger.

Brack frowned. "Do you think I could get away with it again?"

"Tell me something, boy! Did the doctor get a good look at your face?"

Brack thought hard for a moment or two. "No, he didn't," he said. "He was just too busy."

"There then. I reckon you can get away with it plenty of times, especially if you'm don't use the same medical centre each time."

Brack nodded his head. "You know of someone else who needs a certificate?"

Farmer Jones grinned hugely. "I know plenty of the buggers," he said.

"Twenty pounds a time?"

He nodded. "Twenty pounds a time."

"Who be it?"

"Ah!" said Jones. "What we need's to do is a little bit of business, my boy. For every man I get you to stand in for, you 'ave to give me five quid."

"Five quid! Blimey! That be a lot of money!"

The farmer leaned encouragingly towards him. "Think of it this way, my lad," he said. "I 'ave me contacts. They know and trusts me a plenty. They won't know who you be, though. I promise you that you will make fifteen out of the twenty quid every time."

Brack frowned, for this seemed all too easy. "I don't know, seems I be giving you a lot of money."

"Ah! But 'tis I that will be taking all the risk. All you'm 'ave to do is go for the medical and bring the certificate back here. If you ever get caught, all you'm 'as to say is that you want to serve your country so badly that you are prepared to run the risk of dying in training! Every bugger who hears you say that will think that you be a hero! Besides, every time you do I'll give you fifteen quid and as much cider as you can drink. We can go on forever!"

Brack grinned, the greed obvious in his eyes. "Deal!" he said. "When do you want me to go again?"

Farmer Jones grinned happily. He took out a piece of paper from his wallet. "On here is written the name of the next man you 'ave to impersonate, he explained. "On it be 'is home address, 'is parents name and where 'e lives, plus a few other personal details."

"Why do I need that?"

23

"Because, me boy, we need to be a little smarter than anyone else, that's why. Look upon it as if we be going into business together, like. We need to study up on these few details. Be you up to it?

Brack's eyes lit up at the thought of the potential money he was about to earn. "You definitely got someone waiting for me to impersonate then?"

"No," replied the farmer. "I got about twenty of the buggers needing a certificate!"

"Twenty! Christ almighty, that's a lot of money for me!"

"Yes, about three hundred pounds. And there'll be more of 'em coming too!"

Brack chortled aloud. The thought of all that untaxed cash coming in made him feel deliriously happy. He took a deep gulp of the wonderfully cold cider and swallowed it down. It seemed to go straight to his head. The farmer smiled too – for he was charging his customers forty pounds for each certificate!

Historical note: The dark and austere days of World War II were looming starkly upon the horizon and the government of the day decided that it had to act decisively and quickly. It was begrudgingly admitted by those in power that all of Britain's current armed forces and reserves could not possibly meet the manpower requirement in the event of an all-out war.

On the 27th April 1939, Parliament passed the Military Training Act. This legislation introduced conscription for all men inclusively aged from 20 to 21 years old. They were now compelled to undertake a mandatory six months military training.

On the outbreak of the Second World War, Parliament passed the National Service (Armed Forces) Act. This meant that all men between 18 and 41 were made liable for conscription. It was also announced that single men were to be called up before married men. Some hasty weddings were suddenly arranged.

You Just Got to Eat - January, 1940.

January 1940 was the coldest month that had ever been recorded in Britain since 1895. It had been snowing on and off for a couple of days but it was not quite yet settling on the ground. Unbeknown to the British public, nature had created a unique and special set of circumstances that was due to wreak havoc throughout the land.

It started simply enough. Snow began falling extremely high up from a level of cold air. As it fell, it passed through another level of air, but this was a warm one. It turned the spiralling snowflakes into drops of rain. As the rain tumbled down from the sky they hit another, but shallower layer, of cold air. This froze the rain, giving it no time to turn to sleet or snow. As it hit the cold ground it turned instantly into ice. This unique set of circumstances had a terrible effect on the land and because of the storm the effect on the wildlife and flora was catastrophic.

"Bloody hell!" said Tony, rubbing his cold hands fiercely together. He was 14 years of age and the elder of the two brothers, so he was grown up enough to swear. He shivered and wrapped his scarf tightly round his neck. The box he was carrying over his right shoulder and suspended by a linen strap purloined from a gas mask haversack, bounced freely against his youthful body as he moved slowly across the treacherous sheet of ice that covered the field. The wooden box had air holes in the top. Within the box, and anxiously waiting to be released, was a huge yellow and black polecat ferret.

His 11-year-old little brother, Peter, slipped and fell. "Bugger!" he shouted vehemently as he bumped the ground hard, bottom first.

Tony laughed. "You be alright?"

Peter got gingerly to his feet and ruefully rubbed his sore behind. "That hurt!" he complained.

Tony laughed again. He glanced towards the sky and commented, "Strange old day innit, Pete? I've never seen weather like this before."

"It iced up bloody quick," his brother responded, feeling sort of grown up as he used the mild swear words that he often heard his brother use.

The two boys moved carefully onwards. The grass was frozen and it crunched noisily beneath their feet as they trudged down towards the rabbit warren at the far end of the field. Old Farmer Grimble didn't mind them hunting his rabbits; in fact, he actively encouraged the boys. His farm was plagued with them and they could quickly munch their way through a growing field of Red Standard wheat in a remarkably short time.

Meat was rationed and scarce in these frugal times, particularly in the towns. Living in the countryside it could be easier found. A good rabbit would fetch at least a shilling at the local butcher's shop in Yeovil.

There was a deep ditch on their left, and along it grew a high hedge interspersed with trees. The boys were expertly casting their eyes about, concentrating on the area around them to look out for the tell-tale signs of rabbits, their droppings. Suddenly there was a loud explosion behind them. They spun around to witness a Willow tree dramatically splitting itself in half. The sheer weight of the ice on its branches from the storm had caused this to happen.

"Bugger me!" exclaimed Tony.

"Bloody hell!" agreed his little brother. "I thought for a minute 'twere a bomb going off behind us!"

At the bottom of the field there was a pond surrounded by Willow trees and partially obscured by a large bramble bush. It usually had some Mallard ducks in it so the boys already had some handy sized stones in their pockets. Not that they usually had any luck in bringing down the fast flying and shy birds as they rose speedily into the air, but still; you never knew.

They silently approached the pond and heard the familiar "quack quack" of the ducks, although the noises they were making seemed that much louder than usual. Each boy held a stone ready, for they knew that as soon as they walked out from behind the blackberry bush the ducks would fly away.

Putting the ferret box down quietly on the ground, Tony indicated his readiness to Peter by nodding his head. He held his fingers up to three and then put one down, making the countdown to zero. As soon as the last finger went out of sight, both boys sprung out into the open, their hands raised and ready to throw the stones.

There was a panicking series of "quacks" as the ducks furiously flapped their wings to make good their escape. Instead the two boys looked on in utter amazement as five ducks tried to fly off, but they could not. The sudden ice storm had frozen their legs into the water.

Peter threw his stone. It cracked the ice around one of the ducks, but did not break it. Quickly he reached for a replacement from his pocket.

Tony put his hand out and stopped him. "Hang on, Pete!" he called urgently. He pointed towards the flapping ducks, his voice shaking with excitement. "Them buggers be caught! They can't fly away!"

Peter removed his boots and his socks. There was no way he was going to let these ducks and such a bountiful source of wonderful food escape. He knew that although the pond was quite big that it was no more than a foot in depth at its deepest part. Although the ice had slightly cracked because of throwing the stone, it demonstrated that it could not be very thick and it would probably not support Peter's weight.

Gingerly he reached out with his right foot and pushed all his weight down on it. It took some effort before the ice splintered and broke, showing it to be about a quarter of an inch thick. Peter took a sharp intake of breath as his foot entered the water. "God's truth! 'Tis bloody cold!" he grumbled.

Carefully the young lad started walking out across the pond, breaking the ice gently as he made his way slowly towards the trapped birds. Luckily, they were not very far out from the bank, a matter of only 10 feet or so.

"Careful, Pete!" his brother called. Tony passed Peter his stick, skilfully sliding it across the ice to him. His younger brother picked it up and got within reach of the first duck. Choosing his moment carefully, he struck the duck across the back of the head and

27

instantly killed it. He dispatched the four others in quick succession. Breaking the ice around each bird, he released them. With a victorious look on his face Peter waded back to shore, his prize booty held firmly in both his hands.

Throwing the dead birds down onto the grass he swiftly put on his socks and boots. "Bugger me," he said to Tony as his elder brother quickly tied some string around the legs of the dead birds. "My feet are blooming well freezing!"

"Twas worth it Pete," replied Tony. "Mum will be over the moon with this lot."

"Bet she sells a couple of "em up the pub so she can get some cider!" was the uncharitable, but true, answer.

 The polecat ferret caught the smell of the blood that the ducks had spilled and it went into frenzy, scratching the sides of the box with its claws in a futile attempt to escape.

Peter stamped his feet on the ground to get warm whilst Tony cut a thick willow stick with his trusty jack-knife. When he had finished, he passed one end of it to Peter, who grasped it without a word. Each bird was tied on to the stick, and like that the two lads walked on down towards the rabbit warren, their prizes suspended from it.

The bounty was not to end there. They came across two fat pigeons, their wings outstretched with a heavy coating of ice. They were just lying on the surface of the field, still alive but trapped by the ice. The boys realised that they were on to something special here and after dispatching the pigeons laid down their carrying poles.

Quickly scouting around the field the brothers found that other prize birds had suffered the same fate. They collected two pheasants and a partridge and to their utter joy and amazement found a frightened hare fixed firmly to the spot. Tony had to hit the huge animal three times on the head before it finally died, squealing like a stuck pig. Outside of the warren they found three rabbits firmly iced into the snow, but alive. They were soon not.

All the dead birds, the hare and the rabbits were tied to the stick which fairly bent under the weight of their trophies. There was no need to call on the skills of the by now highly agitated polecat ferret. They had enough bounty. Struggling manfully, the two boys carried their prizes home to an astounded mother. That night there was plenty of meat on the table for a change. The hare would be hung up in the garden shed for a week or two for the meat to cure and to reduce the game taste of it. Then the family were in for a rare treat. Mother would cook a Jugged Hare. And mother did earn some cider.

Historical note: This ice storm really occurred and the consequences of what happened were well chronicled, but not until after the war. The scale of the ice storm was subject to strong censorship for the enemy not to gain any advantage from it.

Trees were rent asunder because of the weight of the ice and power lines suffered the same fate. Roads were turned into ice rinks and a greater number of car accidents happened which was far more than those that normally occurred at that time of year.

Even birds in flight were suddenly forced down with the weight of the ice that had almost instantly accumulated on their wings. Pheasants, partridges, rabbits and hares, to name but a few animals, really did get frozen into the ground. This devastating arctic ice storm lasted for two days.

A Jug of Cider - 1st June, 1940.

For Great Britain, the dates between the 26th May and 4th June 1940 marked the deepest defeat inflicted upon her for many a year. It was an extremely decisive beating that was turned into a victory of some sorts as the bewildered and bedraggled men of the British Expeditionary Force were withdrawn over the killing ground of Dunkirk. Men were dragged off the beaches by an assortment of little ships that rescued many of them out of the sea; wounded, wet through and miserably cold. At the same time, they were being constantly machine gunned and bombed by enemy aircraft, with brief respites being given by the arrival of a rapidly diminishing number of British Hurricane fighters over the scene. When they finally arrived at the beach, the men had a better chance of getting picked up and taken away by the assortment of little boats that somehow managed to survive the attention of the Nazi dive bombers.

Tom Storrie, of the Bedfordshire Regiment, was one of those lucky men who managed to get away. From the little boat that had safely brought them back across the channel to Dover Harbour, Storrie and the little group of survivors with him had been helped into a waiting lorry. From there the packed vehicle had taken him and other wounded men to the train station at Dover, a short distance away.

He was sitting down on a packed wooden bench, exhausted, waiting for someone to tell him what to do next. His right arm was in a sling and his shoulder hurt like blazes. A German bullet still lay lodged within it. Men sat around and waited for something to happen; falling asleep in whatever position they happened to be. Storrie marvelled at the way it was possible for men to sleep soundly, but still standing up.

After what seemed like an age Storrie noticed some medical staff making their way purposefully along the crowded station platform. A tall man with a stethoscope hanging around his neck was looking at each of the wounded men. When he had finished, he would rapidly give instructions to one of the many nurses that seemed to be accompanying him. Behind them came a welcome sight, ladies with pots of tea! At last the doctor's slow procession reached him.

"What happened to you, my lad?"

"I managed to stop a jerry bullet in my shoulder, sir."

The doctor gingerly pulled back the first field dressing that covered Storrie's wound and peered intently into it. With a pair of scissors, he swiftly cut away the back of his battledress and then his shirt. "You're lucky," he said. "The bullet does not seem to have gone in too far. It looks as if it was almost spent by the time it hit you."

"Lucky? I thought I was damned unlucky, sir!"

The doctor grinned, his teeth gleaming white in comparison to the blood-stained jacket that he wore. "Yes, private. You are very lucky indeed compared to some of the others around you," he said. Kneeling he deftly removed the sodden shell dressing and triangular sling. Peering intently into the wound he put his hand around to the pretty nurse who stood behind him without even looking at her. "Forceps!" he said curtly.

The nurse smiled and handed the doctor the instrument he had asked for. "Here you are doctor."

"Now, brace yourself, private. I don't have time to give you anything to kill the pain but I can see the bullet. I'm just going to pull it out. This is going to hurt."

And hurt it did, but Storrie just grimaced as the doctor probed briefly around inside the wound. He gave a triumphant smile as a complete 9-millimetre bullet head was successfully extracted. "There you are, what a little beauty," he said. Holding the bullet head up to the light he examined it. "It's complete, lucky for you. Here," he added, and dropped the spent bullet into the private's hand. "Present for you." He turned to the pretty nurse beside him. "Dress the wound and get him on the next train out, wherever it may be going."

"Yes doctor." She smiled sweetly at the private. "Now you will start to feel a little bit better, I hope."

A little old lady appeared behind the nurse. "Do you want a cup of tea, luv?"

Storrie laughed. "Is the Pope catholic? My darling, I've almost swum the channel to get one!" Then he passed out.

The old steam train rattled noisily and shook from side to side during the long night. Everywhere wounded men were moaning, some crying out in their physical or mental anguish. Somewhere Storrie heard a man forlornly calling for his mother. Storrie slept the sleep of an exhausted man, sometimes waking up abruptly as the head of the man next to him slumped upon his wounded shoulder. He did not curse him, for he knew cursing would do no good. He had seen plenty of dead men at Dunkirk.

The crowded train eventually spluttered to a protesting halt, escaping steam announcing that it had arrived somewhere. Storrie could hear some muted voices outside the carriage windows and the door to his carriage was suddenly pulled open. The black-out blinds rattled as they were let up by a smartly dressed military policeman. A sergeant stuck his head in through the carriage door and said, "All right me lads. Those of you who can, get up and walk out on to the platform. You are where you should be."

Someone said, "And where the bloody hell is that?"

"You are in Yeovil."

"What county are we in?"

The military policeman who opened the door was surprised at the stupid question. "Why, God's county of Somerset, of course."

Some wag spoke from the corner of the carriage. "Abandon hope all ye who enter here."

"Come on then. Enough of your buggering about, you lot! Let's be 'aving you, we've got plenty of work to do." The sergeant pointed at the man next to Tom and said sharply, "Wake that man up!"

Tom shook his head and said simply, "I'm not God."

The sergeant blustered, "Do as I say or I'll put you on a fizzer!"

The carriage, filled to the brim with twenty men, went silent. Storrie gave the man a stony look before he replied. "Haven't you seen a dead man before?" he asked quietly.

The sergeant gulped. "Alright, I'm sorry. Just get out lads." This time he seemed to have a note of pity in his voice. Of the twenty men packed into that one carriage only fourteen walking wounded got out. The sergeant let them make their way outside, helping them where he could. He saw that the men were physically and mentally exhausted so decided to take a different approach to them.

He gently explained, "Look lads, you are at Pen Mill station in Yeovil. I'm going to take you across the road in a minute to the Pen Mill Athletics Ground. Doctors and nurses are waiting for you there, along with other administrative staff. They are going to sort you out. O.K?"

Tom spoke for the others, regretting his sharp outburst at the senior non-commissioned officer, for he was only doing his duty. "Thank you. I'm sorry that I spoke so sharply to you just now."

The sergeant nodded his head. "Nay lad," he replied sympathetically, "you were quite right to reprimand me so."

The sergeant walked them out of the station and Storrie suddenly realised that it was daylight. Shut up in the carriage with the blackout blinds down he had not known what time of day it had been. The men were ushered into a large reception tent where once again doctors and nurses tended to their wounds. Each man was given a tag with his name, number and regiment recorded on it. It also showed their wounds and what treatment they had undergone thus far.

When that was done, they were put into small groups according to their injuries. Then a reedy little clerk took down their regimental details. He looked at Tom and said, "The Bedfordshire Regiment, what's left of 'em, are being relocated to Houndstone Camp. It looks like you are going to be discharged into their tender care."

"The Bedfordshire's? Here?" said Tom excitedly, for he had honestly thought that they had all been killed and that he was one of the lucky ones to have escaped.

The clerk took off his spectacles and started to polish them with his handkerchief. "They are coming in dribs and drabs, but they are here though."

"How many of them are there?"

"About a hundred or so I reckon - so far."

Storrie grinned broadly. He had some good mates in that unit and he had been hoping against hope that at least some of them had pulled through.

The Pen Mill Athletic ground was a combined football and rugby pitch. There was nowhere for the men to sleep, but the playing surface itself was covered in camp beds, a hundred and fifty in a line, two feet six inches apart and eighty across. On each bed, there lay a feather pillow and a rough horsehair blanket. Most of the camp beds contained sleeping men.

At some of the camp beds men were being dutifully attended to by nurses; other men slept the sleep of the dead. A few were. The stench of rotting flesh and untreated wounds permeated the air so that curious passers-by were seen to hold handkerchiefs to their noses. Down the far end of the field lay some men wrapped in their blankets and completely covered. For them, the war – and life, was over.

In the distant background, he heard someone say, "Find yourself a camp bed after you have got yourself some food lads. Go up that end by the pub and you will find a field kitchen has been especially set up for you. Eat as much as you want."

Storrie suddenly realised that he was hungry, very hungry. He tried to remember when he had last eaten a freshly prepared hot meal, but he couldn't. He wandered up towards where he could see a queue of men and gratefully took his place in it. At the head of the queue he could see someone handing out a cup and a knife, fork and spoon. They also handed out a deep tin plate.

At last it was Tom's turn. The man handing him his eating utensils was a civilian. He nodded towards the injured soldier's shoulder. "Hard luck lad, but welcome back."

Storrie smiled, appreciating the warmth of the man's welcome. He said, "Thank you."

At last he came to the head of the queue and three cooks from the Royal Army Service Corps were there, dolling up the food. First, a slice of thick fried bread was unceremoniously dumped upon his plate, the cook using his fingers to do so. Then a good spoonful of wonderfully thick kidneys cooked in beautiful smelling gravy were placed upon the top of the bread. Last of all, and something he really appreciated, a lovely fried egg topping it all off.

He moved away from the queue and sat among the men in a vacant spot on the grass. No-one spoke. Like Hyenas in Africa who were not sure when their next meal would be, they all shovelled the food down as fast as they could. It disappeared as fast as a German U-boat that had been sunk by British destroyers.

A man with a ruddy cheek appeared amongst them, a large brown earthen jug in his hand. He looked towards the men and nodded towards the steaming cups of tea that each man held. He spoke in the soft Somerset drawl and with a usage of vowels that, unless you were used to it, were hard to follow. "I knows that you have some tea there me boys, and this be a tad early in the morning, but in this yer jar I 'ave some scrumpy. Anybody want any?"

Storrie threw his tea away. "I'd appreciate some," he said. The farmer smiled and topped up his warm mug with the cold cider. "When you'm be finished with that, me lad, come back yer for some more if'n you'm want it." By way of explanation he added, "In the first shout I was in the retreat from Mons. Imagine it must have been the same for you at Dunkirk." The old farmer looked about him, a thoughtful look upon his face. "I know what 'tis like, my boys. I lost a lot of my bloody mates there as well. Don't deny it! But remember them with honour. Take a drink in their memory, but only in their memory. Don't let the drink rob you of your reason and respect! Draw a line in the sand and move on."

The eyes of Storrie began to moist up. He remembered how at the bridge just before Dunkirk his lifelong friend, George Worcester from Bristol, had been laughing and joking with him as they checked the charges that had been set to blow it up. A sudden and long burst from a Spandau machine gun had literally cut his best friend in two. The weird thing was, although George was dead by the time he hit the ground, he was still laughing. That haunted him. At that moment, he realised what the old farmer was getting at. Smiling, he proffered his empty mug back towards him.

After they had finished eating they were taken to a large tent and told to take off their clothes. Lying around were several huge tin baths full of wonderfully hot water and the naked men were made to take a quick wash, standing in them. Tom ruefully saw that his poor feet were swollen and that the blacking from his boots had penetrated his skin. Four men got into each bath, and sharing the harsh army issue soap they set about washing themselves. After they had soaped up other men showered away the soap's lather from them by dousing them with cold water from large watering cans. All modesty was forgotten, but the female nurses, young and old together, did not seem to notice the naked men.

Tom winced as he raised his arm to allow cold water to be poured underneath his arm pits. Blood seeped from his wound and went into the bath. It was then he noticed that most of the bath waters were red from seeping blood. Getting out of the tin bath he was handed a large damp green towel to dry himself, one that had been previously been used by someone else. They were then ushered through into a connecting tent where they were given a generous dousing by men donned in protective white clothing and masks. White D.D.T. powder was sprinkled liberally over the hairy parts of each man's body before he was led away into another tent.

In that tent some wooden trestle tables had been set up and behind each one stood a man with some part of a uniform stacked high in front of him. At the first table, they were given a vest and pants to put on, followed by a pair of woollen socks. At the next table, they were given the once over by an experienced man who handed them a pair of denim trousers, and then a denim battle dress blouse. At the end of the tables were crates of boots marked up in their correct sizes. Tom selected a pair of size 8 boots and got himself dressed. He had difficulty in putting on his puttees because of his wound, but one of the uninjured soldiers quickly gave him a hand to wrap the two yards of brown material around the top of his boots and the bottom of his denim trousers.

Within five minutes he found himself outside of the tent with other men. A corporal organised them into ten ranks of three. Calling the men to attention, he turned them right and gently guided them out of the Athletics Ground through two magnificent stone pillars guarded by a pair of wrought iron gates. As they approached the gates, a military policeman opened them for the troops.

They passed beneath a small horse-chestnut tree and turned right, walking up the road a little way. Across the road, they could see a public house, called "The Royal Marine." To Tom's surprise when they came opposite the pub the corporal brought them to a halt.

"Right turn!" he ordered. The men did as they were told. "Stand at ease!" he barked. "Now then, in the skittle alley of this here pub you will find thirty camp beds, one for each of you. The pub landlord and his missus will sort you out with a blanket and pillow in there. You will be sorry to know that you are billeted in there, temporarily, until we can sort out things. The paymaster will be along shortly to give you some back pay. In you go."

The men needed no second bidding and quickly made their way through the myriad of small bars and into the skittle alley. Each man found a camp bed and slumped down on to it. The thoughtful landlord and his wife had already put a blanket and pillow on each bed, so all the men had to do was to sit down on them. Quickly they did what all good soldiers do. Why stand up if you can sit down? Why sit down if you can lie down? Why lie down unless you can sleep? And sleep they did.

The Dance - 2nd July, 1940.

It was a warm Saturday night in July, one of those gentle breeze evenings when all felt right with the world. The sun was still out, although it was starting to gently sink into the western skyline and turning a fiery red as it did so. A steady stream of animated soldiers were making their way along Preston Grove, and outside the St. Andrews Church Hall an orderly queue of them had already formed. They had to pay to get into the dance. Groups of giggling women made their way past the men and into the hall. For them, the dance was free.

Sergeant Alec Horwood and his mate, Tom Harvey, both Queens Royal Regiment, joined the patient queue of men to await their turn to enter. From inside a band struck up and a Master of Ceremonies called out loud enough for all outside to hear, "Ladies and gentlemen. Take your partners please for a Quick Step!" Happy laughter could be heard from inside the hall and the band began to play.

Conversation in the long queue ceased for a moment as they were suddenly reminded that they were at war. A lone Seafire, black smoke trailing from its badly misfiring engine, staggered low across the sky to make an emergency landing at the nearby Westlands airfield. The chattering men were quiet as they waited to hear the fate of the fighter aircraft. There was no explosion, and they gave a collective sigh of relief at its safe landing.

"Hurry up!" called an impatient soldier from the rear of the queue, breaking the captivating spell of the moment.

Another group of young women walked up the path to gain entrance to the hall. One fair haired girl eyed the young sergeant speculatively and gave him an inviting look. Alec grinned back and the young girl demurely cast her eyes down, smiling as she did so. Tom gave Alec a familiar nudge in the ribs with his elbow. "I think someone likes you!" he said, nodding his head towards the departing girl. At that moment, she glanced back again and giggled to one of her friends. Alec's face went a deep red.

He was a tall, good looking young man with the familiar short back and side's haircut that could not hide his fair hair. He sported a clipped military type moustache to try and hide his youthful features, but in this aspect, he failed miserably. He wore a medal ribbon on the left breast of his battle dress blouse, the crimson, dark blue and crimson stripes marking him down as a man who had won the Distinguished Conduct Medal. He was a seasoned veteran.

Alec and Tom paid their shilling entrance fee and entered the packed church hall. There was hardly room to move with soldiers predominantly on one side of the hall and the local girls sitting facing them on the other. The girls were in their best outfits, but already rationing had hit hard and some of the dresses had seen better days. Alec anxiously scanned the hall for the girl he had seen while he had waited in the queue, but to no avail. He passed a searching look to his chum who just shook his head. "Take your partners for a waltz!" urged the Master of Ceremonies and he turned back to conduct his small orchestra, raising his baton as he did so.

Alec felt a gentle tap on his shoulder. "I hope you are looking for me," she said sweetly. Taken aback, he did not know what to say. The girl laughed and took his hand, leading him on to the crowded dance floor. "My name is Madeline," she offered.

He blushed. "Alec. Alec Horwood," he said.

The girl gave a dazzling smile. "Pleased to meet you, Sergeant Alec Horwood," she said in a gentle tone.

They danced through the massed crowd and he thought she felt as light as a feather, never minding when he once stepped on her toe and mumbled an abject apology. The music played but Alec hardly heard it. The band stopped playing, and she laughed gaily as she said, "You can let me go now. The music's finished."

Hastily Alec pulled his arm away from the young girl's waist. Madeline laughed again, and taking his hand walked outside with him. "It's too noisy in there to talk," she explained. She found a handy spot on the stone wall that went around the church hall and took a seat on it. She patted to a spot beside her and said, "Take a seat, Alec Horwood, and tell me all about yourself."

Sitting next to her he said, "There's nothing much to tell, really. I come from London. The war started, I joined up, and now I am here."

She said teasingly, "Are you glad to be here?"

Alec looked down and scuffed the ground with his polished boots. "I am now," he said.

Madeline's face took on a thoughtful look and she said, "Look here, I don't want you to think that I act this way with every man I see. It's just that there is something about you, Sergeant Alec Horwood that I like. And whatever it is, I like it very much."

Embarrassed, Alec gave a little cough. He looked at her and said, "And I like you very much too!"

She pointed at the medal ribbon on his chest. She asked him, "How did you get that?"

Alec reddened slightly. "Oh, it's nothing," he said.

She gave him a stern look. "If you want to see me again, Alec Horwood, you had better learn to tell me the truth when I ask a question, whatever the truth is!"

He closed his eyes and remembered something that he would never forget. The air was thick with circling German aircraft, particularly the dreaded Stuka dive bomber. Its harsh scream from its siren sent men scuttling for safety as they dived to attack the British positions around the outskirts of Dunkirk. Sergeant Alec Horwood had been ordered to defend the position to the last man. "I can't stress to you how important it is for you to give us as much time as you can, Sergeant Horwood," explained the colonel of the regiment. "But for each minute you can hold up the Germans, more men can get off the beach."

Sergeant Horwood nodded. "I understand, sir," he said.

The colonel looked his sergeant in the eye, for he was without doubt going to lose the best soldier he had in his regiment. "You realise that you won't be coming back with us, don't you?"

Sergeant Horwood gave a determined look. "Don't you worry about me and my men, colonel. We know our duty and we will defend this spot to the bitter end."

The colonel reached down and shook the sergeant's hand. "Goodbye, Alec," he said.

"Goodbye sir." The rattle of an enemy machine gun diverted the sergeant's attention away from his colonel as he ran to join his men. He jumped into one of the prepared trenches and, picking up a rifle from one of his dead soldiers, joined in the battle. A screaming Stuka released a bomb, covering the trench with dirt and stones. The man next to him, Scrivens, gave a groan and sank back into the trench, his left shoulder spurting blood. A wave of enemy infantry, supported by tanks, came at them. It was just a matter of time.

The young sergeant tended Scrivens as best he could but the wound was deep and severe. An officer helped him and luckily it was not too long before an advancing German medic knelt to help them. Reaching into his first aid haversack the German pushed a field dressing on to the wound, both front and back. Expertly he bandaged the man up.

Another German soldier indicated to the two men that they should now leave their care. Standing up, both men put their hands on their heads and started to dismally walk towards certain prolonged captivity and the end of the war for them both.

Probably the last artillery shell fired in the defence of Dunkirk suddenly exploded virtually next to the German and his prisoners. After the searing blast of the detonation and the whizz of shrapnel had passed, the sergeant found that he was alone with the captain who had been helping him. Of the German, there was virtually no sign, except a left boot with a bit of leg sticking out of it. A large pool of blood soaked the road indicating that the German soldier had taken the full force of the blast. Looking around, Alec saw that the coast was clear. "If we're going to make a break for it, it's time we did so, sir," he said.

The captain nodded. "Let's go," he replied.

For two weeks, the two men followed their way along the coast, and just outside of Antwerp a friendly Dutch seaman found them and took them out and into the English Channel. Here a passing destroyer found them and took them aboard. They were probably the last two men to escape from the retreat of Dunkirk.

Alec gave Madeline a boyish grin. "It's not something I like to talk about," he said, pausing. "But perhaps someday, to the right lady, I might."

Madeline smiled and took his hand. "I think I might be the right lady," she smiled. "Come on. Let's go for another dance!" Laughing, she raced ahead of him and slipped back into the dance hall. Alec followed behind, a warm glow in his heart.

Historical fact: Sergeant Alec Horwood was awarded the Distinguished Conduct Medal for his escape and on the 28th December 1940, was commissioned as a Lieutenant in the Queen's Royal Regiment (West Surrey). He married his sweetheart, Madeline Dove, of Yeovil in April 1941. On commissioning, he was attached to the 1st Battalion the Northamptonshire Regiment and was serving with them in 1944 when he was killed in action. For his outstanding act of bravery, he was awarded the Victoria Cross.

LEST WE FORGET

HORWOOD, Alec, Lieutenant, V.C., D.C.M.

The Balloon Goes Up - 7th October, 1940.

Sergeant John Delaney of the 957th Squadron, Royal Air Force, sat at a table on which rested an old and battered black field telephone. He was carefully studying an engineering manual about balloon construction and relaxing on that Monday, the 7th day in October 1940. The war had started over a year ago, and he had joined the Royal Air Force in high hopes of becoming a flight engineer with the rather grandiose idea of serving his country by taking the fight directly to the enemy.

He had begun well in the RAF and had been swiftly promoted to Sergeant as a Flight Engineer on one of their bombers. He had eagerly looked forward to the sheer joy of going up in an aircraft and this happened quite quickly. His long-awaited expectation then rapidly turned into one of absolute terror as he discovered that once above 500 feet something unexplainable happened. The pressure on his ear drums inside the aircraft caused him to curl up in abject misery and pain. A hastily abandoned training flight ensured that any chance he ever had of flying again would never take place. The Medical Officer had grounded him – permanently.

He now commanded one of the 24 Low Zone Kite Balloons that ringed the Westland Airfield in Yeovil. John was the senior non-commissioned officer in charge of the Yeovil Number 16 site. This was inside the Westland Aircraft Works itself and located at the end of the main building. This factory was vitally important to the war effort. It made the new Whirlwind fighter plane, as well as some Spitfires and Hurricanes. In addition, it also manufactured the Westland Lysander aircraft, the little aircraft that was so widely used for British clandestine operations.

One of the real consolations of the job was that at lunch times some of the pretty girls from the assembly line would always come over and sit on the grass near the site to eat their lunch, weather permitting. One of them, Sally, seemed to be particularly fond of him, and he of her. Today he would pluck up enough courage to ask out her for a date.

Delaney's real pride and joy was the silver coloured beauty of a barrage balloon that he oversaw. When it was fully inflated, it was about 64 feet in length and its height rose to a majestic 31 feet or so, at least so the manual said. The diameter of the balloon could be measured at round about 24 feet, but this fluctuated slightly depending on how much hydrogen gas was pumped into the beast.

The conscientious Non-Commissioned Officer was reading the section of the manual explaining that the material used to make this balloon was a two-ply rubber proofed Egyptian cotton. Each piece was finished off with a black undercoat of waterproof paint and then given an aluminium varnish topcoat. It took 600 pieces of this material to make his balloon, for he considered it "his" balloon, for the thousand square yards that constituted each two-finned blimp that ringed the airfield.

The balloon itself had two compartments, separated by a gas proof seal. Occasionally a panel would tear and one of his men, Jock Wilson, would sew the new panel in place, quietly muttering obscene curses as he did so. Sometimes enemy aircraft would attack the balloon, causing bullet holes in it that needed to be made good, which he did not mind so much.

What made Jock Wilson grumble most was the tiny holes caused by birds pecking at the outside of the balloon. They were hard to locate but caused just as much hydrogen loss as a tear a foot long. He honestly believed that the colour of the balloon attracted small insects. Birds would peck at the insects that settled on the balloon, thereby causing lots of tiny and nearly invisible holes to appear. When something occurred that Jock Wilson couldn't repair, they would collapse the balloon and drive it across to the Barrage Balloon Repair site based in the St Michaels Hall in Yeovil itself, next to the church in St Michaels Road. There was also part of a Polish Ambulance Brigade based there.

When this daily inspection was completed it had to be recorded. The sergeant had been doing this every day for the last six months, and to be quite honest about it he was getting tired of this mundane and boring duty.

44

Every day the barrage balloon had to be rigorously checked. Once a week an officer would come over from the 957 Squadron HQ based at Braggchurch House on Hendford Hill. He would then personally carry out the inspection and heaven help the crew who presented a neglected balloon. They never knew on what day the inspection would take place, but he knew that the Squadron Leader would not visit today as he was officially on a long weekend leave. He had the petrol rations to do it, thought Delaney bitterly, and not without some jealousy.

Sighing heavily, he stood up and glanced out of the window of the little hut in which he found himself. The Fordson Sussex winch lorry stood about twenty feet away from him. When the warning came, it would be up to him to rush over to the lorry and start the winch, letting it out so that the tethered balloon would rapidly rise to its maximum height of round about 7,000 feet. This would be on a calm day and it would attain height quite quickly. The 0.31 of an inch diameter steel cable would tether it safely into position.

Contrary to popular belief, it was not the lorry and the winch that held the balloon in place. Admittedly the winch controlled the ascent and descent of the balloon and the lorry played a large part in guiding it, but in reality, the steel wire ran from the lorry to a main anchorage that was sunk into the ground. This consisted of a cubic yard of concrete that weighed in at around two tons. He grimaced as he remembered how a couple of months ago a high wind had torn the lump of concrete out of the ground, but luckily they had managed to retrieve the balloon without much damage having being done to it.

At the North Weald airfield in Kent, 23-year-old Sergeant Pilot Douglas Nicholls walked carefully around his Hurricane Mark 1. His name was painted in white in small letters beneath the cockpit. His aircraft, P3154, was fully fuelled and ammunitioned up, ready to meet the constant threat of the German aircraft that were making a daily appearance.

The aircraft belonged to 56 Squadron RAF and was part of the Duxford Group. It seemed to Nicholls as if he was always in the air

and fighting for his life. Today had somehow been slightly different.
The sergeant had been hanging around since midday, and now it was
getting on towards late afternoon. He reflected that he would rather
be in action than waiting around for something to happen. Nicholls
decided that perhaps inaction was not as exciting as real action after
all.

In the ready room at Middle Wallop airfield, Pilot Officer Michael
Staples of 609 Squadron RAF was discussing tactics with his
wingman, Sergeant Pilot Alan Feary. Both men flew Hurricane Mark
1's. All the pilots in the ready room were officers, except for
Sergeant Feary. Rank didn't matter with them, for they were all
pilots and as such they ate, slept and fought together. The only time
when rank arose as an issue was when a senior officer visited the
unit. Relationships between the non-commissioned officer and the
commissioned officers would immediately revert to a "Sir" and
"Sergeant" basis. Once the visitor had gone it would just as quickly
relapse to first name terms.

That afternoon throughout the West Country it seemed as if, for
the very first time, the Germans would not come. Already someone
had dubbed the current air war as "The Battle of Britain" and Pilot
Officer Staples thought it aptly named.

Deep below the ground in a bomb proof shelter, Air Vice-
Marshall Brand sat in his chair at the control room of Number 10
Group and thoughtfully stroked his chin. The air was thick with
cigarette and pipe smoke. Looking down he watched carefully as his
officers and non-commissioned officers placed model enemy planes
on the table over France, using wooden poles with a flat end to move
the aircraft plot forward as the new position of the enemy aircraft
was reported. One of his wing commanders looked down at it and
said to the Air Vice-Marshall, "Looks like Gerry has got something in
mind for us, sir."

Air Vice-Marshall Brand nodded sagely and quietly bided his
time. He was waiting for the sudden dash that the enemy would
inevitably make towards the coast. Then it would become a bit of a
guessing game as to which direction they would go. It could be up

the coast towards London, or down the railway line towards Exeter? Maybe they would head straight across to Bristol?

He leaned forward as one of his pretty female WAAF's pushed a group of model aircraft onto the channel part of the map painted on the huge table below him. The enemy aircraft were just over the Cherbourg Peninsula. Watching closely, he saw the plotter push the aircraft across the coast at St Albans Head. "It's Yeovil they're after!" he muttered to himself. He turned towards his wing commander and said in a matter of fact tone, "Scramble 152, 238, 601 and 609 Squadrons."

Sergeant Nicholls had just returned to the ready room when all hell broke loose. At each of their respective bases telephones shrilled their urgent message, "Squadron scramble!"

The telephone rang. Delaney gave an involuntary start, surprised at its unexpected ring. He grabbed the black telephone and holding it to his ear quickly spoke into the mouthpiece. "Number 16 balloon site!"

A calm voice came over the telephone, "Air raid red!"

"Air raid red? Yes sir!" Dashing outside Sergeant Delaney called out loudly to his team, "Air raid red!" and his balloon team reacted without thinking. Half a dozen of them ran to the tethered balloon and began to release the ropes that held the balloon steady on the ground. In about thirty seconds the sergeant had reached his lorry, and, deftly leaping on the back of it had confidently stabbed the starter button of the petrol driven winch with his index finger. The powerful engine roared into life. At the same time the balloon was released from its moorings and it began to soar upwards in a steady rate of climb, under control of the carefully watching sergeant at the winch. Being such a calm day it did not take long for the balloon to reach its maximum height.

There had never been a really successful air raid on Yeovil yet, apart from the one in July that put some bomb craters in the grass runway at Westlands. The sergeant did not run as quickly as he could have, neither did his crew. To them it had the appearance of just another exercise.

Young Joyce Brown looked out from her bedroom window and saw the barrage balloons rapidly ascending around Westland's airfield. She shouted, "Looks like that a raid's coming mother!"

From downstairs came an urgent reply. "Quickly love. Follow me into the shelter."

Rushing down the stairs the young Joyce grabbed her thick coat, for she did not know how long this raid would last. All she knew was that the men at the barrage balloons got the warning first before the air raid wardens and that it would be a minute or so before the air raid sirens in Yeovil would be sounded. They had ignored the warnings when they first heard them that July, and she and her mother had nearly paid the ultimate price. They had run screaming for shelter as enemy aircraft really did appear and bomb the nearby airfield. Now they took every warning as a real one.

Joyce ran through the open door of the Anderson Shelter that was dug down into the rich dark earth that comprised the back garden of Seaton Road in Yeovil. Her mum already had the primus stove burning with a kettle full of water on it. The sixteen-year-old girl closed the door behind her and sat down on the bed made of wooden boards. Outside, the sirens began to wail.

"Do you think it really is a raid this time?" she asked.

Her mother shook her head from side to side. "I don't really expect so. The last dozen or so times have all been false alarms, but it's better to be safe rather than sorry."

"I hope that this is a false alarm too!"

At Barwick Park, just outside Yeovil and towards Dorchester, the heavy anti-aircraft guns began to fire.

"Oh, dear me," said Mrs Brown. "I don't think that this is going to be a false alarm, luv."

Twenty-five JU88 bombers of Kampfgeschwader 51 (Edelweiss Squadron) (KG51) (Battle Wing 51) and accompanied by fifty Bf110 twin engine heavy fighter aircraft from the Zerstörergeschwader 26 (ZG 26) (Horst Wessel Squadron) steadily droned towards the little market town of Yeovil, a sleepy little hollow that until this moment had never really experienced the totality of war. The Squadron's mission was quite simple. Their orders were to blow the Westland Aircraft factory off the face of the map.

The incoming bombers and their fighter escorts had been picked up some ten minutes earlier as they crossed the English Channel at Weymouth and turned towards their target. British Hurricanes and Spitfires had been scrambled and were being hurriedly vectored towards Yeovil to give combat against the invaders. Number 152 Squadron RAF, based at Warmwell in Dorset and equipped with Spitfires, met with the attacking force within minutes of taking off. They headed for the bombers and were soon intercepted by the Bf110 fighter aircraft.

Forty-six-year-old Reginald Batstone and his fifty-seven-year-old wife were out shopping that day, albeit that the shopping was been done very reluctantly on Mr Batstone's part. The couple lived at the nearby village of Stoke-sub-Hamdon, about some five miles distant. On a whim, they had decided to catch the bus into Yeovil to try and buy some much needed items. The ration book they shared was held securely in Florence's old leather handbag and they were idly meandering up Middle Street. Their gentle stroll was interrupted as the strident and banshee wail of a warning siren suddenly rent the air.

Air raid sirens had occurred a few times before but nothing had really happened, apart from a few air raid wardens shouting dire threats at them because they were not taking it seriously enough! Reg Batstone, by this time, had more than enough of shopping without buying anything. His wife had been trying to find herself some blue cloth and found that what she needed had far exceeded her allowance in her ration book. Despite this she still insisted on looking around in every shop she possibly could. Reg just wanted to go home and have a cup of tea. The shops were closing anyway and he was looking forward to the taste of a lost pheasant that a friend of his had provided, for a price of a couple of pints of cider, of course.

"Come on love, we got time to get the bus if we hurry!" cajoled an impatient Reg.

"No dear," replied his wife sternly. "I've got a bad feeling about this."

Reg looked at her, concern in his eyes and a moment of doubt in his voice. "Don't you worry old girl," Reg assured his frightened wife. "Nothing's happened before when the sirens have sounded."

His wife looked up at him, her calf eyes widening in the late afternoon sunshine. "Reginald! I'm really scared. It doesn't feel right!"

Reginald Batstone comfortingly patted the thin arm of his wife, which by now had forcibly linked up with his. Reg could feel her trembling beneath the rough serge jacket that she wore. "Now, now, my love!" he consoled. "It won't do us any harm at all to take shelter this time. Let's treat it as a practice!" He said the latter in a gay tone, hoping to reassure his nervous wife. Reg was not sure about this, for his wife had earned a strong reputation in the local women's circles. She was a bit of a clairvoyant and it was not unusual for her to predict something that no-one else had. She had warned anyone who had listened to her about the disaster at Dunkirk a month or so before it had happened.

Gratefully Batstone's wife glanced up at him, a palpable sigh of relief escaping through her mouth. "Yes, my darling," she said. "Let's just do that!"

Reg smiled, for he did love this woman, but sometimes she did get frightened so easily. He patted her on her arm again in pure affection. Pointing across the road he said in a confident voice, "Let's pop across the road and shelter in Burtons. We should be safe enough in there."

Florrie laid her head on the comforting arm of her husband. "Do you think we should?"

Reg kissed the top of his wife's auburn covered head. "Of course we should my love! Have I ever got it wrong?"

Stepping up to her full four feet eight inches in height she gave her husband a little peck on his cheek. "I'd trust you with my life, darling." She gave a happy, radiant smile as they both crossed Middle Street and descended the stairs into the air raid shelter beneath Montague Burtons tailors shop. She felt safe and secure.

Above and behind the JU88 bombers the Spitfires of 152 Squadron RAF from Warmwell got themselves into a prime attacking position. The Squadron Leader gave a shout of, "Tally Ho!" and the Spitfires arrowed down from the cloudless blue sky. They were amongst the enemy bombers in a moment, firing their machine guns as they did so.

The bombers quickly took evasive action and scattered, leaving one of them to fall behind trailing a plume of smoke as it turned around and tried heading back to the safety of France. Number 152 Squadron was quickly joined by Number 601 Squadron from RAF Filton. Whilst the Spitfires from Warmwell concentrated on the bombers, the Hurricanes from RAF Filton attacked the Bf110's, forcing them away from their prime role of protecting the JU 88's. To survive, they had to. Everywhere single combat in the form of dog fights started to occur, but the leading bomber led his flight steadfastly forward, jinking and diving to avoid the attacking Spitfires.

The pilot had a general disposable bomb load which consisted of an internal load of 10 in number SC-50 kilogram bombs, 2 in number SC-500 kilogram bombs carried under the inner wing hard points and 4 in number SC-250 kilogram bombs on the four outboard hard points. Everything told each JU 88 bomber carried about 2,000 kilograms of high explosives.

The navigator of the aircraft pointed forwards and said to his pilot, "Target ahead!"

The pilot acquired the town of Yeovil in his vision as it lay straight to his front. The radio operator opened fire as a Spitfire flicked by them, guns blazing. The captain of the enemy aircraft dropped his nose and went into a steep dive for about two hundred feet before levelling out again. The aircraft filled with the acrid smell of gun smoke and the captain made ready to drop his bombs.

He shouted to his navigator, "How many aircraft are still with us?"

The co-pilot swivelled around in his seat and looked backwards. "About ten bombers!" he cried excitedly in his heavily accented Austrian voice.

"Thank you. Get yourselves ready. I'm going to be releasing my bombs soon."

The aircraft droned on and got itself on a level path at about 250 miles per hour. This was always the dangerous time for a bomber; the moment the pilot flew in a straight and steady line was the moment of the greatest danger. As if to confirm this, sudden puffs of smoke started to appear around the aircraft. There was a pinging as spent anti-aircraft fragments from the four inch shells that the British fired pepper-potted the approaching aircraft.

There was a louder bang and a scream of pain came from the radio operator. A sudden rush of incoming air told the pilot that they had sustained a hit behind him. He yelled, "Franz!" but there was no reply.

The navigator shouted, "Bastards!"

The pilot stabbed his finger at the bomb release button and automatically called out over the intercom, "Bomben los!" In response, his aircraft suddenly lurched upwards as the heavy bomb load that the plane was carrying was suddenly released. With its twin engines roaring, the aircraft clawed for height just as it passed over the Westlands airfield.

Sergeant Nicholls stabbed the firing button on the round spade grip of his Hurricane fighter plane and a stream of bullets from its eight .303 machine guns slammed into a JU 88, breaking pieces off it. The aircraft rapidly lost height and he moved in for the kill. The next thing he experienced was the jerking of his aircraft as a Bf110 fired into him from close range. He cried out in agony as a bullet passed through his arm and at the same time gave thanks to God that the rear of the seat carried armour plating. He had felt a couple of bullets bang into it, but thankfully they never came through. The engine of his aircraft coughed and spluttered and the area around him began to fill with a dense, black smoke. Petrol poured into the cockpit and rapidly covered his feet. At the same time the controls of the aircraft became sluggish and it began to invert itself, covering him in the gushing fuel that came somewhere from in front of the instrument panel. Sergeant Nicholls knew that he had no options left. Throwing back his canopy with his one good hand he released himself and dropped out from the doomed aircraft.

He let himself fall clear of the combat zone before he tugged frantically at the ripcord. It was not unknown for German fighter planes to strafe parachuting pilots. With a satisfying tug, the canopy of his parachute opened. Beneath him he saw his inverted aircraft crash into the ground at the village of Alton Pancreas, exploding as it did so.

The ground rushed up to meet him and he landed safely, but injured. As he hit the earth his ankle twisted and he heard it snap. Thankfully he slipped into unconsciousness. That was how the farmer found him before gently loading the wounded airman on to the back of his empty trailer and rushing him towards the main road and further help.

Pilot Officer Staples led the attack on the bombers with his wingman, Sergeant Feary, following closely behind. It was a textbook approach with Staples getting off a good burst that ripped into the side of a JU 88. Sergeant Feary, following closely behind, also got a burst in on the aircraft. Flames poured from its starboard wing and it hastily jettisoned its bombs, turning in a half circle to make its way back to France. A Bf110 and his wingman came hurrying after the two Hurricanes and opened fire. In accordance with a well-rehearsed plan, Staples broke to port and Feary to starboard, making the two-attacking aircraft unsure as to which one they should pursue.

A couple of Messerschmitt Bf109's suddenly appeared from somewhere and Pilot Officer Staples flew right into them at 1630 hours. Before he had time to react, the Messerschmitt's had hit him, and hard. The Hurricane immediately caught fire, and with a bullet in his side the wounded pilot immediately bailed out.

Sergeant Feary had seen what was happening and had vainly tried to turn to help his leader. As he watched the burning aircraft bank away steeply to the left and out of control he was gratified to see that a parachute blossomed out above the doomed plane. Then he saw the Messerschmitt's turn back towards his leader. They were going to machine gun him! Diving steeply, he put his Hurricane into an almost vertical aspect, praying that he could get to the enemy aircraft before they reached Pilot Officer Staples.

Thankfully he did and gave himself a satisfied smile as he saw the leading plane stagger under the impact of his bullets. He watched his friend land safely and turned back to combat. The sky was empty now and he rolled around to starboard to seek a target. From out of nowhere an enemy aircraft fired upon him and his plane lurched crazily away and went into a spin. Fighting hard to regain control he rapidly lost height, but the enemy aircraft that had fired into him had his own problems with another Hurricane from 609 Squadron.

At last he regained control and found himself streaming smoke and flying low over Dorchester. He decided to land at Warmwell but then to his horror found that he could not lift the nose of his aircraft. It was doomed. Rolling over, he dropped out of his cockpit and pulled the ripcord of his parachute.

At 300 feet, the parachute did not have time to fully open and Sergeant Feary plummeted to his untimely death. His aircraft crashed at the nearby Watercombe Farm, Warmwell.

The bombs rained down on Yeovil, reaching from Middle Street across to the airfield itself. Mrs Batstone looked skywards as the high-pitched scream of an approaching bomb seemed to pinpoint the exact spot where they were cuddled in each other's arms. A devout Christian and a member of the Salvation Army she felt no fear. "Oh Reg," she murmured softly. In a brief and blinding moment, Mr Montague Burtons Fifty Shillings tailor's shop disintegrated, killing the Batstone's and six other persons.

Major Wolfgang Hess of Kampfgeschwader 51 (Edelweiss Squadron) was flying the lead bomber that had led the attack on Westlands airfield. He was pulling hard on the stick, giving maximum thrust to the two Junkers Jumo engines. Suddenly there was a horrendous noise from the port engine. Glancing towards it he saw it entangled in a steel wire.

The navigator pointed skywards and said in a horrified tone, "Oh my God!" They had hit a barrage balloon and the two men had grim looks on their faces as the forward momentum of the aircraft pulled the balloon inexorably towards them at a high speed. They thought that the balloon was about to explode above them and that would be the cause of their deaths.

On the ground, Sergeant Delaney saw the JU 88 collide with his balloon. For a moment, the cable went taut as it sent a tension wave up along it. He watched in relief as the cutting links exploded 150 feet above him. He knew that the same tension wave would also explode another cutting link 150 feet from the balloon. His crew cheered as they saw this happen, and at the same time a parachute attached to each of the cutting links deployed. This action would release the barrage balloon so that it could be located and reused later, but also at the same time the force of the two parachutes would act as an irresistible force against the enemy aircraft. It would crash.

Major Hess and his navigator both sighed in relief as they saw the balloon suddenly rise and break away. That relief was only momentary as the balloon's parachutes deployed. The effect of the drag was instantaneous. The plane was immediately dragged into a deep dive to port and it began to invert itself. To many, that would have been the end, but Major Hess had been a pilot for twenty years and his experience in flying aircraft was without parallel. He had also been a test pilot before the war and so he reacted calmly to any situation. He gently rolled the aircraft over on to its back and began a loop. The port Jumo engine was silent and still, the blades of the propeller having been ripped away by the force of the 0.31-inch steel cable that had tethered the balloon.

An anti-aircraft site they were passing over opened fire at them and the cockpit took a huge impact. Acrid smoke filled the space around the pilot, but luckily for him the impact had also blown away the Perspex on the navigator's side and had created a large hole. The contaminated and smoked filled air was sucked out through it, as was his unfortunate navigator.

Cursing loudly the major fought with the controls of the crashing aircraft. He had steeled his mind to dying and had calmly accepted death, but he was not going to give up without a fight. The hard drag to port was still pulling him towards the earth and so he rolled his aircraft to port. Miraculously, the cable fell away from the damaged engine and aircraft wing. He somehow managed to get himself back on an even keel. He glanced up, a bead of sweat running down from the bottom line of his leather helmet to his eyes. He dared not wipe it away as he needed all his strength wrestling with the control stick. The major saw water ahead of him, but at the same time also recognised the island of Steep Holme in the Bristol Channel. He had bombed Bristol three times already so he had used that island as a navigational aid before.

He glanced helplessly to where his navigator should have been. The poor man had the one thought to escape and had unbuckled his seat harness ready to bail out. The huge hole in the side of the plane had sucked him out. The pilot hoped that the navigator had remained conscious enough to have pulled his ripcord of the parachute. It was then that the major noticed that part of the parachute harness was still attached to what remained of the seat. He also noticed the huge amount of blood there.

Shaking his head, he concentrated on the task at hand. That was to keep flying and keep airborne. His air speed indicator had dropped considerably and the controls were becoming harder to handle. Smoke was pouring out from his port engine although the trusty Jumo engine that remained seemed reliable enough. He found that he had a choice to make. The major could ditch the aircraft and bale out, or he could head for home. He heard a groan from behind him and knew that his radio operator must still be alive. Professional pride made the decision for him. He headed for home.

A lone Spitfire of 609 Squadron RAF spotted him. Climbing up into the sun the experienced pilot studied the JU 88 while it slowly staggered its way across the sky as it headed for home and safety. The British pilot was not without compassion. He came down out of the sun, but seeing the state of the damaged aircraft elected not to open fire. Instead he flew past the badly damaged JU88 and waggled his wings, the signal for his foe to surrender.

Major Hess would have none of it. He vainly fired his frontal machine guns after the departing Spitfire in the forlorn hope of hitting it, but he didn't. The Squadron Leader sighed. He flew above and behind the JU88 and in two five second bursts saw the aircraft crash into the countryside, exploding on impact.

That raid had cost the German air force 2 JU88 bombers and 7 Bf 110 escort fighters lost in action. The toll would have been more exacting for the enemy had not a squadron of Bf 109's been despatched to help the enemy forces as they retreated. Five British aircraft were lost and two were badly damaged.

His barrage balloon was recovered intact the next day, much to Sergeant Delaney's joy. He cursed inwardly as he saw the damage it had sustained, but then smiled to himself, knowing that he and his crew had done their job, and done it well.

Historical note: This raid on Yeovil, first on a Somerset town, occurred on this day. Killed in the Vicarage Street Methodist Church were: Mrs F. LUMBER, Mrs W. BRIGHT, Mrs V. PICKARD and Mrs M. BUGLER. Killed in Messrs Burtons were: Mr R. BATSTONE, Mrs F. BATSTONE Mr A. PALMER, Mr F. ROSE, Mr N. GAY, Mr W. TUCKER, Mrs E. SMITH and Mrs L. JOHNSON. Killed in Summerleaze Park was Mr C. RENDELL from West Coker. Killed at 25 St Andrews Road was Mrs A. HAYWARD. Killed at Grove Avenue were Mr L. FORSEY and Mrs M. MORRIS.

LEST WE FORGET

743201 Sergeant Pilot Alan Norman FEARY, aged 28
Number 609 Squadron RAF
He is buried at the Holy Trinity Churchyard in Warmwell, Dorset

Lufton Camp - 14th October, 1940.

To the west of Yeovil lay the sprawling Lufton Army Camp, a mixture of hastily constructed wooden huts thrown together with some stone buildings to house a huge wartime community. Within the camp a large ammunition store had also been established. Only two days before, on Saturday the 12th October 1940, the German Luftwaffe had paid an unwelcome visit, dropping their bombs on the camp opposite Houndstone. On that Saturday afternoon, four soldiers lost their lives in the raid and many more were injured.

Lieutenant Colonel George Frederick Richard Wingate OBE, Royal Artillery, stood in the darkness of the room and peered out of the crudely painted green iron windows of the Officers' Mess, an almost empty china tea cup with a gold rim held in his hand. Ruefully he gave thought to how long it would be before the windows before him were repaired properly. The last enemy air raid had blown out several of the small nine by nine inch glass window panes. Such was the scarcity of glass that an orderly had replaced the missing panes with hastily cut out pieces of wood from empty ammunition boxes, some of which did not quite fit properly. As if to remind him of this, a gust of cold winter air rattled one of the loose pieces and it made an irritating noise.

He frowned. It was time to go to work. Sighing, the colonel finished his drink of lukewarm tea and placed the empty cup on the little table that stood next to the window. He drew the blackout curtains firmly across the window and touched a Bakelite light switch. Three naked electric bulbs suddenly gave a dismal light to the room and threw dark and mysterious shadows into every corner. The Colonel walked purposefully across the mess ante-room and out into a small corridor.

A piece of batten wood had been screwed into the wall and on it protruded little iron pegs. On one of these was his Sam Browne belt, the traditional officer's belt, complete with a sword in its scabbard, and his peaked cap. He lifted his belt off the peg and put it on, breathing in a little so he could tighten it an extra inch or so. It made it appear as if he had a narrow and trim waist.

His cousin, a colonel named Orde Wingate and the Commanding Officer of an anti-aircraft unit, had laughed at him and said, "It's no good tightening your belt like that, George! You need to get off your fat little bum and run it off!"

George Wingate had glared at his cousin, for he did not like being told the truth. He did not have the time to follow a rigorous fitness regime. He was too busy being the Commanding Officer of Houndstone Camp.

Once he had put his belt on he gave his sword a little lift to ensure that it slid out of his Sam Browne belt easily. Not that he needed it, of course, but it was by now a force of habit and second nature to him. Taking down his cap, he took out the brown cape gloves that were concealed within it. He placed his hat firmly on his head, checking in the mirror to ensure that it was set square. He grunted in satisfaction, pulled on his gloves and looked at his watch. It was a quarter to seven in the evening, and outside it was dark. He moved along the corridor, holding his sword handle and pushing it down and away from him. That would ensure that he did not trip over it when he was walking.

The colonel entered the Officers' Mess reception room and the duty corporal sprang to attention. Besides him a sergeant wearing a red sash also drew to attention and saluted his Commanding Officer. "Sergeant Speight, Duty SNCO, reporting as ordered sir!"

"Good!" grunted the colonel. "We are going to make a few surprise visits around the camp, sergeant. Have you a note book and pencil?"

The sergeant patted his battle dress blouse. "Always have one on me, sir!" he said.

The colonel nodded coldly. "I would expect you too, sergeant. Follow me."

The colonel walked past the sergeant and stood by the door, the Senior Non-Commissioned Officer closely in attendance. "Put the light out," he ordered curtly.

The Orderly Corporal switched off the light. The Duty SNCO pulled back the blackout curtains and opened the door for his superior officer. They waited for a little while so that their eyes could adjust to the dark. When he was ready, the colonel led the way.

Monday the 14th October 1940 was a grey and overcast day with patches of drizzle occasionally pitter-pattering off the black tarmac runway of the captured French airfield. The Do17 lay glistening in the dusk as the German officer walked around the outside of the aircraft, inspecting his "Fliegender Bleistift (flying pencil)" in the fading light. The officer frowned as he affectionately patted the aircraft's wing, for he did not like the fact that his aeroplane glistened, reflecting some of the last light. He must have a word with his engineers and have the camouflage re-painted. A glistening aircraft is an open invitation to an attack. He had already flown 20 battle missions and he wanted to be around to do many more.

Tonight, he would take off in the dark at 1815 hours. On the previous Saturday, he had been part of a group that had attacked the Westland's airfield in Yeovil, Somerset, but had been forced away by British fighters. He had dropped his bombs on the secondary target of opportunity on that Saturday and the local German agent had reported that the bombing of the camp had resulted in the deaths of some army personnel.

He smiled in satisfaction as he recalled how he had been told in tonight's briefing that his target would be a single aircraft attack on the large and sprawling army camp that lay on the outskirts of Yeovil. A big ammunition compound had been pointed out to him by the Intelligence Officer on an enlarged air photograph. He was to try and hit that, if he could.

He again carefully studied his map of the area, for he wanted to make sure that he did not hit the nearby Prisoner of War Camp. His younger brother, Fritz, was being held there, captured during the very first week of the war against England. Fritz had been unlucky – he was strafing an English convoy in France when an unexpected Spitfire pounced on him from behind, shooting him down so that he had crashed in front of the very convoy he had been trying to destroy. Apparently, the Tommie's had not been amused by the German pilot's attack on them. Some of them had treated Fritz very badly with the result that his younger brother had been hospitalised for two months. Not because of any injuries sustained by him when he had brilliantly crash-landed his aircraft, but rather because of the actions of the aggrieved British soldiers.

Sergeant Speight rolled his eyes heavenwards as the colonel's shielded torch pointed accusingly towards a pinpoint of light that shone through a blackout curtain in one of the offices. "Sergeant!" he said firmly. "Go and sort it out. Meet me in the guardroom in 10 minutes."

"Very good, sir," he said. He cursed inwardly because he knew that one of Wingate's little foibles was any blackout violation. Sgt Speight guessed that the colonel would now have "one of his famous moods", and anything could happen. He hurried across to the offending building, and, knocking on the door, entered.

Once inside he closed the door behind him. Drawing back the door's blackout curtain he entered the office, his eyes taking a moment or two to get accustomed to the light. An elderly sergeant major looked at him curiously.

"Excuse me, sir," the sergeant said politely. "I'm doing rounds with the colonel and he pointed out that a small light is showing through your blackout curtain."

The sergeant major gave a groan. "Oh God!" he blasphemed. "Trust the colonel to spot that!" Looking directly at the Orderly Sergeant he asked, "What's his mood like?"

"I dunno really, sergeant major. He didn't come across here and speak to you himself so that is something, I suppose." As he spoke Sergeant Speight saw the offending crinkle in the curtain and smoothed it out, blocking out any escaping light. "There! That should do it."

"Thank you."

"I'll go outside and check it for you."

The sergeant major nodded his head as the Orderly Sergeant disappeared behind the heavy blackout curtain of the door. The door opened and he heard Sergeant Speight close it behind him as he went outside. After a moment, there came an urgent rapping on the window. "It's all O.K. out here now sergeant major!" called the Orderly Sergeant.

The sudden wail of the air raid warning rent the air. "Bugger it!" exclaimed the sergeant major as he reached for his steel helmet, hoping that it was not the chink of light from his window that had caught the enemy's attention. Placing it deftly upon his head he carried on making out the guard duty roster for the rest of the week.

Hauptsturmführer Otto von Schultz sat at the controls of his light bomber, the Dornier 17 E-1. He had already checked communications with his three crewmen, the bomb aimer/gunner and his two other gunners. All non-commissioned men, they were keen and eager to take the fight to the enemy and attack Britain.

The two BMW VI 7.3 12 Cylinder liquid cooled in-line engines gave a powerful roar as the aircraft strained against the brakes that held it still. A green light flashed twice at the end of the runway. The hauptsturmführer (the equivalent of an RAF Flight Lieutenant) released the brakes and the aircraft surged forward, its weight being at 7,000 kilograms', just a bare 39 kilograms' short of its maximum take-off weight.

The aircraft hurtled down the runway, gaining speed with every metre. It had almost used the entire length of the runway before it finally became airborne. At that moment, von Schultz retracted the undercarriage and the engines quietened a little as the drag was reduced. Swiftly it climbed up to 4,000 metres before the pilot banked gently and set a course for England.

The one thing the hauptsturmführer liked about attacking Yeovil was that navigationally it was very easy to find. All he had to do was fly straight across the channel to Lyme Regis, then over to Exeter and follow the railway line up to Yeovil.

As he approached the coast he increased his height by another 500 metres, just to confuse the anti-aircraft gunners if they thought they had him in their sights. No flak came to meet him, although he was expecting some.

Over the outskirts of Exeter, he swiftly saw the reflection of the steel rail lines of the main Exeter to Waterloo line. He did not even need this, for a train was steaming up the line, sparks flying from its smoke stack. "You just as well have shone a torch for me," he grinned to himself. He flinched as flak suddenly erupted around him, but as suddenly as it had come, it went.

The pilot carried only one High Explosive 500-kilogram bomb. The other 500 kilograms of the bomb load consisted of incendiary bombs. The maximum safe permitted bomb carrying weight for his aircraft type was 997 kilograms', but as it was war time this was very often exceeded.

Feldwebel Karl Schultz, and no relation to the pilot, spoke calmly into his intercom. "How much longer to the target is it, captain?"

"Getting into position now, Karl. Probably about another 5 minutes flying or so I would think. We shall be making a left turn and then another left turn. I'll let you know when to get ready to release our "babies". Both men laughed.

The wailing of the air raid siren caused the colonel to move a little faster than he was accustomed to. He hastily entered the guardroom to be met by a surprised corporal. The Junior Non-Commissioned Officer hastily jumped to his feet, guiltily placing a large white earthenware cup full of tea down on the desk in front of him. A lance corporal sitting next to him closely followed suit.

"Alright men, relax!" the colonel said, a smile on his face, and he waved his hand at the men to indicate that they should sit down again.

The two NCOs eyed each other and the corporal asked in a worried voice, "Do you think they are after us, sir?"

The colonel shook his head. "No, probably Westland's again," he reflected in a reassuring tone. Then as an afterthought he added, "But you can never be sure."

In the distance the heavy anti-aircraft guns based in the grounds of Barwick House opened their booming barrage against the Hun intruder. Sergeant Speight was almost at the Guardroom when the guns began to fire. Turning around he glanced up into the night sky and saw the white puffs of exploding shells contrasting sharply against the darkness. Then he heard the noise of a single aircraft approaching coming from the direction of the centre of Yeovil. He dashed inside the guardroom, displaying a chink of light in his haste. He saw the colonel and blurted out, "The bugger is coming straight at us sir! I think that we are in for it!"

"Right men!" spoke the colonel calmly. "Quickly, get on the floor now, all of you!"

The four men threw themselves down on the wooden floor and heard a whistling bomb, its high pitch scream getting louder with every moment. Colonel Wingate put his hands over his ears and curled up into a protective ball. This bomb would not miss!

Historical note: At 7 o'clock on the evening on the 14th October 1940, a lone raider dropped his bombs on Houndstone Camp. The attack killed 18 soldiers and wounded another 48. The ammunition store was set ablaze but thankfully most of the ammunition was physically moved before the fire could ignite it. The consequences of a fire consuming the ammunition would have been horrendous for Yeovil, and there would have been many more casualties. Several huts, a garage and part of a nearby YMCA were destroyed or damaged.

Buried in the Soldier's Plot in Yeovil Cemetery are six of the casualties from this attack. Every year, in a separate ceremony after the main Remembrance Day parade, the Yeovil branch of the Royal British Legions gathers at Yeovil Cemetery to pay their respects to these soldiers, and the others that lie in peace there.

LEST WE FORGET

1634916 Gunner Patrick COFFEY, Royal Artillery, aged 25.
1565165 Gunner John Thompson PALLISER, Royal Artillery, aged 32.
798451 Sergeant Sydney George SMITH, Royal Artillery, aged 27.
34792 Sergeant George SPEIGHT, Royal Artillery, age unknown.

12404 Lieutenant Colonel George Frederick Richard WINGATE, Royal Artillery, aged 56.
15024666 Lance Bombardier Francis Alan Dudley WOOD, Royal Artillery, aged 22.

U.X.B. - 6th November, 1940.

Lieutenant Duncan Adam was old for a lieutenant, for he was aged thirty-seven years. Well, you would have thought that at his age his rank would have been much higher than just a lieutenant, but in truth he had been in the Army for 19 years already. He had risen through the ranks in the normal way and had reached the position of a Staff Sergeant in the Royal Engineers when war had finally broken out in 1939. He had been at Dunkirk and had proved himself a handy man when dealing with explosives. On board the destroyer that had rescued him, he had been brought to the notice of his superiors when he had successfully defused a bomb that had not exploded but had penetrated deep into the bowels of the ship.

For that action Duncan had been promoted from the ranks and had been made a full lieutenant. It was now Wednesday the 6th November 1940 and he was had become an expert in his field, defusing unexploded bombs.

Lance Corporal Charlie Andrews, the 20-year-old driver provided to him by the Royal Army Service Corps, pulled up outside the Officers" Mess at Houndstone Camp in his one ton Bedford utility lorry. He beeped three times on the horn to let his officer know he had arrived. Corporal Francis Lilyman threw back the rear tarpaulin cover of the truck and nimbly jumped out. Putting his hand into his trouser pocket he took out an envelope that he had collected from the Operations Room. It would be their task for the day.

Lieutenant Adam came out of the Officers' Mess and strode briskly towards the waiting truck. Corporal Lilyman threw up a salute which was returned by the officer. The lieutenant cheerfully greeted his men with, "Good morning Francis! Charlie!"

"Morning sir," they replied in unison.

The lieutenant stretched out his hand towards the Royal Engineers corporal. He smiled at his right-hand man and his erstwhile assistant in any bomb disposal task. The corporal handed him a buff covered envelope with "Lieutenant Adam RE" scrawled across it. Swiftly he opened the envelope and read the typewritten instructions inside. Glancing up at his two men he said, "We're to go

66

through Chilthorne Domer towards Ilchester to a place called Oakley House. Apparently, there is an unexploded bomb there left over from the hit and run raid on RNAS Yeovilton last night. Looks like they missed by a mile!" he grinned.

The two soldiers laughed and the corporal got into the back of the vehicle. Lieutenant Adam hauled himself into the passenger seat. Sliding back a connecting piece of glass on the back of the cab he called through to the back of the vehicle. "Everything secure back there Frannie?"

The face of the corporal suddenly appeared by the window. "Right as rain, boss. Let's go!" he replied. The driver, Charlie Andrews, smiled. They were a very tight knit group, the three of them, and discipline was a little bit different when they were working together as a team. Gone was the formal "sir". From now on until completion of their mission Lieutenant Adam would just be addressed as "boss", unless a senior officer suddenly made an appearance and that was highly unlikely. They tended to stay clear of the Bomb Disposal Team when they were dealing with an U.X.B.

Oakley House was easy enough to find for a policeman was waiting on the main road to direct the bomb disposal squad towards the place. It was a large house on the left-hand side and roughly halfway between Chilthorne Domer and Ilchester. Charlie Andrews had looked longingly towards the Halfway House Inn as they drove past it in the forlorn hope of catching a glimpse of his new girlfriend, Betty.

He had met her only on that Sunday evening and on that Monday, they had shared their first kiss which had quickly led on to some heavy petting. "Oh, my goodness Charlie!" she had excitedly gasped, extricating herself away from him, at the same time replacing her loose bra. "What sort of girl do you think I am? I never go this far on a first date." She had patted her hair back together and promised, "Maybe on the next date we'll have a better time?" She giggled meaningfully and waved him goodnight as she retreated into the inn through the servant's door, closing it securely behind her. He was going out to see her tonight and he couldn't wait to get his hands on her.

A private of the Home Guard stopped them as they pulled into the driveway of the house. The dishevelled youth of about 17 years of age threw up what he thought to be a perfectly executed salute as the one ton vehicle came to a halt and the officer got out.

"You be here about that there bomb, I 'spect?" he commented in his broad Somerset accent.

Lieutenant Adam smiled, for the Somerset accent always amused him. He was a Jordy from Tynemouth himself. "Aye, my bonny lad. You are right about that!"

The Home Guardsman smiled to himself as he thought how strange the officer's accent sounded. He could hardly understand him. "Follow I, then, zur," he said. Slinging his .303 rifle over his right shoulder the private of the Home Guard walked on down the drive of the house, stopping at a small gate that led into a field. "It be over there," he said, pointing towards a mound of piled up dirt.

Lieutenant Adam nodded towards the house and said, "Have the occupants been evacuated?"

"Yus, they 'ave been. They buggered off just after the bomb was dropped. Fair scared "em zumthink zilly, it did too!"

The lieutenant nodded his head. "Well, that's hardly surprising. Right then, let's get started, shall we?" he said cheerfully, rubbing his hands together to get them warm.

They had to remove the little gate from its hinges and break down one of the posts to drive the truck through to the hole in the field. Charlie drove the vehicle up to about ten feet away from where the bomb had burrowed itself into the field and turned off the engine. As the truck stopped, so Frannie threw out the picks and shovels that would be needed to dig it out. Duncan took out a long expanding rod and carefully pushed it down the hole until it contacted the tail fin of the bomb.

He inspected a mark on the metal rod. "It's about 15 feet down boys," he said. "From the look of the size of the hole I would say we are dealing with a 250-kilogram bomb."

The corporal had picked up a spade and had already started digging. The lieutenant removed his battledress blouse and undid the top button of his battledress trousers, his leather braces supporting the weight of them. He picked up a pick-axe and waited. Frannie would move out of the way when he needed a breather or hit something solid.

The ground was surprising easy to dig and they did not need to resort to any heavy equipment. They dug carefully, making a round hole about five feet in diameter. The hole was in a sort of "V" shape, angling down towards where the bomb lay. Occasionally the officer would reach down into the hole with his hand to clear away the loose dirt that had fallen in it.

Whilst they were digging, Charlie was busy filling sandbags with the removed earth. He made a circle around the two men as they dug and quite quickly the hole was surrounded by the sandbags. They were placed alternately, like brickwork, around the hole. One layer would be placed lengthways, pointing towards the hole, and on top of that layer another two would be placed but in the opposite direction. This gave the sandbags some strength and would protect those on the outside of the unexploded bomb should the worst occur.

Whistling a tuneless song, Charlie placed the black field telephone on top of the sandbags and ran the black cable from it back to the driveway of the house where he placed it upon a wooden trestle-table. While the boss was in the hole and defusing the bomb, he would talk to Frannie at the top of the hole and tell him what he was doing. Frannie would then relay what the boss had said down the field telephone line to Charlie who would write everything down. It was a well-practised but important standard procedure and was easy enough to do.

When he had finished doing that, Charlie got out the tripod from the back of the lorry and set it up over the two busy men in the hole. He then rigged up the block and tackle, an essential part of the retrieval system. When the boss was ready, they would place a rope around the tail fin of the bomb and simply pull on the block and tackle to lift the bomb clear and give the boss room to work on it. It was a simple procedure and one the team had used effectively ever since the raids on Yeovil had commenced. This would be the twentieth such bomb that they had dealt with.

The block and tackle was also used to send down a bucket. Whoever was in the hole would fill it up with earth and Charlie would pull it up to the top and empty it. The bucket would be sent back down again and the whole procedure carried out once more.

Frannie came up from the hole, his face covered in dirt. He and the boss had been down there for about two hours now and were almost at the U.X.B. He gave an impish grin as he winked at Charlie. "Boss says to get the kettle on, Charlie. It's time for a cuppa!"

The corporal took over the empty bucket from Charlie and sent it back down the hole. By then the lance corporal had gone to the back of the truck and taken out a primus stove and a kettle. He poured some water from a water container, just enough for three pints of tea, into a black kettle. Pumping up the primus stove he lit it with a match where the finely misted spray of paraffin came out of the nozzle. The little cooker burst into flame and Charlie placed the kettle firmly on it, checking that it did not rock on the primus stove. He did not want it to fall off when it would eventually begin to boil.

He had some lecherous thoughts about Betty as he took out three large one pint tin cups from the wooden box in which they kept their tea things. The large enamelled tea pot, well chipped around the lid and spout from usage, was produced and placed on the ground next to the kettle. Steam was already beginning to spiral upwards from the kettle's spout. From the box, he took out the tin tea caddy that they had been given by a little old lady when they were defusing a bomb over by the Westlands Aircraft Works. He put three teaspoonful's of black tea into the pot, being careful not to spill any. Into each of the large cups he then added two teaspoonful's of sugar. He glanced quickly towards Frannie to make sure that he wasn't looking and secretly added a third teaspoon of the white and valuable commodity into his own cup. He did have a sweet tooth.

When the kettle boiled, he poured it into the pot, stirring it with a large teaspoon. "Tea up, chaps!" he called.

Frannie pulled a bucket of earth clear and called down into the hole. "Tea up, boss!"

Lieutenant Adam stood upright and rubbed his aching back. He scratched his head and said, "I think I can get the rope around the tail fin now, Frannie. Come on down and give me a hand. Get Charlie to man the bucket." Charlie had heard the instructions and automatically came over to stand at the edge of the hole. Frannie went over the lip and down into it as the empty bucket was lowered down. He untied it and put the bucket to one side, handing the rope to the boss. The lieutenant reached down into the hole where the tailfin of the bomb was exposed. It had four fins. Each was connected to one another by a piece of metal about an inch thick that ran from corner to corner of each fin. Expertly he threaded the rope through each of these, grazing his knuckles on one of them as he did so. The lieutenant swore and extracted his hand to give a quick lick to the scrape before putting it back down to the fin to end the job. Once they had lifted the bomb up by a foot or so he would be able to access it through a sealed metal panel. A large screw with a slot in it held it securely in position. He hoped that this would be an easy job as the Germans had started to booby trap a few of their latest bombs.

"There!" he exclaimed, a note of triumph in his voice. "Another one of Mr Hitler's bombs safely roped in and ready for defusing." He looked up from the eighteen feet of depth that they were in and shouted up, "Take the slack off the rope Charlie, and tighten her up. I want to see how she looks." Charlie took the slack off the rope.

They never knew what went wrong. It was just one of those things. The bomb suddenly exploded, instantly killing all three of the men.

Historical note: The U.X.B. did explode and killed the three men who were attempting to defuse it. They all lie buried in the Yeovil cemetery at Preston Road, Yeovil, Somerset.

71

LEST WE FORGET
6th November, 1940

144842 Lieutenant Duncan ADAM, Royal Engineers, aged 37.
T/68220 Lance Corporal Charles William Edward ANDREWS,
Royal Army Service Corps, aged 20.
1870478 Corporal Francis John LILYMAN, Royal Engineers, aged
21.

You'm Different- May, 1942.

It was nearly the fourth year that Britain had been engaged in the world war. The Americans had finally entered the global conflict after the brutal and unprovoked attack against them at Pearl Harbor where Japan had sunk most of her ships of war that had been peacefully anchored there. With the influx of American troops into Britain in this year, an event occurred for which many of the British public were just not prepared. That event was equally as worrying for the Americans themselves.

The American jeep pulled up outside the bank in Yeovil. Three huge white helmeted soldiers leapt out and one of them saluted smartly as the officer in the front seat exited the vehicle. He carried a leather briefcase with a metal chain running from the handle and handcuffed to his wrist. "Wait here," the officer ordered curtly, but in a strange accent.

The men were all over 6 feet tall, their white helmets and cross straps noted them down as men of the Unit Provost. Each man carried a pistol in a white holster on his belt which they unbuttoned with practiced ease as they exited the jeep.

Pedestrians stopped to stare. A young boy looked at one of the soldiers, his mouth agape. The soldier grinned and said, "What you all looking at boy? Nevah seen a soldier afore?"

The boy shook his head from side to side. "I 'aven't seen one like you! You'm different! Who be you then?"

The soldier grinned. "Private First Class Everard Collins, at your service," he replied, bending in a mock bow from the waist and trying to fake an English accent.

"You be black!" the boy exclaimed with a note of incredulity in his tone. "Where be you from?"

The three soldiers grinned at each other, white teeth flashing in smiles that were set in their handsome ebony coloured faces. One of the other soldiers looked at the tan on his arm and said in a mocking, surprised tone, "Well look'e here fellas! I am so!" All three soldiers laughed loudly.

73

The boy pointed accusingly at the jeep. "How come your steering wheels on the wrong side?"

The driver grinned at the boy. "Where I come from, boy, it's in the right place!"

The boy shook his head. "It baint! All of our cars have the steering wheel on the right-hand side of the car!" The boy gave a triumphant grin as he expounded his knowledge.

The driver shook his head. "Over here you guys drive on the wrong side of the road to us. Where I come from, everyone drives on the right-hand side of the road." The boy looked dumbfounded at the reply.

A young girl of about 17 years walked boldly by, smiling provocatively at the driver of the jeep. He gave a startled look to his companions and then smiled back at her. As she walked away, she looked back over her shoulder, her smile giving him an exceptionally inviting glance.

The huge American black man bent down on one knee and addressed the lad, who was about 10 years old. "We've all come to help you, boy!" he smiled. "We're from the good old US of A, come to win the war for little ol' Britain!" He put his hand into his pocket and pulled out a stick of bubble gum. He proffered it towards the boy. "Here," he grinned. "Have some gum!"

With some uncertainty, the boy walked towards the outstretched hand of the American and gingerly snatched the stick of chewing gum away from him. It was wrapped in shiny silver paper. "What do I do with it?" he asked uncertainly.

It was the soldiers turn to look with incredulity at each other. The soldier at the back laughed and said, "Why, unwrap it and chew it, of course!"

The boy excitedly unwrapped the piece of gum he had been given, and placing it into his mouth, his jaws made a chewing motion. His face took on a look of pure delight as for the first time in his life he sampled American chewing gum. His face broke into a huge grin of pleasure. "Bugger me!" he exclaimed. "I like this!"

The driver of the jeep grinned and took out a whole packet from his pocket. "Here boy," he offered. The lad took the pack of chewing gum and hastily secreted it away on his person. "Now skeedaddle out of here!" he was ordered. The boy needed no second bidding and ran off, waving back to the soldiers as he did so.

The young girl made her way back towards the three soldiers, provocatively swaying her hips and twirling her small handbag around in the air. She had seen a recent movie where the American heroine had done the same and too a good effect. She stopped at the jeep and nodded knowingly. "You be Yanks baint you?"

The black driver of the jeep saluted her. "Yes ma'am!"

The girl squealed in delight. "Oh," she gasped, "you be big buggers baint you!"

The three soldiers looked at each other and exchanged smiles. The driver's face took on a serious look. "Are you supposed to be talking to us, ma'am?"

"What do you mean?"

"Well," he said, a note of caution evident in his voice. "You're a white woman and we are blacks."

"So?"

The three men exchanged glances, a curious look etched upon their faces. "Well, where we come from white women just aren't allowed to speak to black men."

The girl snorted in disgust. "I don't care where you be from. I talks to whomever I likes!"

The driver's eyes opened wide in surprise. He grinned at the girl.

"My name's Eileen," she said, "Eileen Mary Dyer."

The soldier saluted her and said, "P.F.C. Everard Collins at your service, ma'am."

The teenaged girl extended her hand towards the startled soldier. "I'm pleased to meet you to be sure, Everard." With a slightly stunned look on his face the PFC reached forward and shook the girl's hand. "Welcome to Yeovil," she smiled, giving the soldier a little curtsey as she did so.

At that moment, the white officer walked out of the bank. He frowned deeply as he witnessed his driver shaking hands with the white woman. "What the hell do you think you are doing, Collins!" he demanded to know.

The driver let go of the girl's hand as if it had been scalded by hot water. He hastily saluted and the other two men drew themselves up to a ram-rod position of attention. "Nothing, sir!" he shouted, his eyes staring straight ahead. "Just being welcomed to the town by this young lady, sir," he offered by way of an explanation.

The officer shook his head. Looking at the girl he said with a note of disdain in his voice, "Where I come from it is not the proper thing for a white woman to be seen talking to Negroes."

Eileen drew herself up to her full 5 feet 2 inches and snorted angrily. "Well, we baint bloody well where you be from! Here I can talk to who I like!"

The officer's face went a bright red, for he was not used to being spoken to like that. He gave his three soldiers a hard look. "Get into the jeep, now!"

The three men instantly responded and the driver turned on the ignition of the vehicle. The white officer got in as the girl walked around to the driver's side. "I like you tanned Yanks," she smiled. "How's about a date with me then, me lover?"

The officer exploded in fury. "Goddamn it, Collins. Drive off - now!"

"Yes sir!" Collins slammed the jeep into gear and pulled away, the tyres of the utility vehicle screeching as he made a rapid departure.

Bessie called after the departing jeep. "What about that date!" With their officer's face set in a stony gaze forward the two black soldiers in the back of the jeep grinned at each other. One of them turned around and waved towards Eileen. Furiously, she waved back.

Historical note: The coming of the black serviceman into Britain had a deep and lasting effect upon their way of life. In the USA, they had usually been treated as second class citizens and even in the armed forces they were not allowed to mix with their white counterparts. Whilst building the American hospital at Houndstone Camp in Yeovil, the black soldiers were bussed in during the day and taken away to tented accommodation out in the countryside at night.

During the evening time, they found relaxation in 'blacks only' pubs and bars. But what changed everything for them was the way that they were treated by the British population. Racial discrimination, although it existed, was not nearly as harsh as it was in America. Consequently, many black men and white girls had affairs, some of them resulting in illegitimate children. These new social experiences had far reaching consequences for when the black soldiers eventually returned home.

Wasted Bread - July, 1942.

Mrs. Mayhew entered the Magistrates Court in Yeovil with an unsure feeling that he had never experienced before. She was a woman of impeccable character and to be summoned to answer to an alleged crime was the most shameful thing that had ever happened to her. She wore what she thought was a most impressive large brown trilby type hat with a red band around it. Two ostentatious Ostrich feathers adorned it on either side. Around her neck was draped a large fox fur, its tail and head dangling down towards her rather plump waist. She wore a brown tweed jacket and skirt with a matching pair of sensible brogue shoes. The magistrates would surely recognise that she was a woman of breeding and that it was a ridiculous mistake to have her arraigned before the court on such a trivial matter. Her maid followed on diligently behind her, her eyes downcast. A soldier gave a wolf whistle towards her servant and Mrs. Mayhew glanced sharply at him.

A young policeman was sitting behind a desk of the main court reception room as they entered. He looked up in some surprise as she strode purposefully towards him. Respectfully, he rose to his feet. "Yes, madam," he said. "How can I be of service to you?"

The lady gave a sniff of disdain. "My name is Mrs. Mayhew," she explained. "I was asked to be here for ten o'clock."

The policeman looked at the list that lay on the desk in front of him. "Are you a witness, madam?" he asked in a somewhat nervous tone, for clearly the lady was of some breeding.

She looked down at her shoes. "I have been summoned to attend," she said haughtily, "on some ridiculous charge which I am sure will be immediately thrown out once I have seen the magistrates."

The young policeman blushed a bright red and starting flustering around with his paperwork. A seasoned sergeant, seeing the young man's discomfiture, walked over and took charge. "Alright PC Bibbs!" he said, in a brisk and authoritative manner. "You go and gets yourself a cup of tea my lad, and I'll deal with this lady." The constable gave his sergeant a grateful look and quickly hurried away from the desk.

Mrs. Mayhew glanced from side to side and noticed that some unsavoury types were looking at her. One had the temerity to grin and then give her a huge wink. She turned her face away angrily. The nerve of the man!

"Where shall I go, sergeant?" she said.

The sergeant looked at the list and took a moment or two to read it. "Mrs. Gertrude Mayhew?" he said.

She sighed. "Of course!"

The sergeant nodded. "You will be called shortly, Mrs. Mayhew. You will be seen in Court One, which is behind the centre door. Take a seat please."

Mrs. Mayhew looked around the holding room for the court. She leaned forward and whispered to the policeman, "You don't possibly mean that I have to sit here, do you?"

The sergeant looked around him. He kept his voice low and reasonable. "Of course I do. Take a seat and an usher will call you forward shortly."

Mrs. Mayhew put her hand to her mouth. She was very embarrassed. She looked with pleading eyes at the sergeant. "I can't possibly sit here with all these, well, ruffians!" she said, throwing her hand around the air in an expansive manner. "Isn't there a private room where I can wait with my maid?"

The sergeant became firm with her. "All defendants have to remain here, madam, and wait their turn until they are called forward into court."

"But.....!"

"I'm sorry madam. No buts! Will you please kindly take a seat." The sergeant thought for a moment, rubbing his chin with his hand as he did so. "You can always remain standing if you want to."

Mrs. Mayhew gave a huge sigh of exasperation. She knew that there was no point in arguing with the man. "Come, Rose!" she said sharply to her maid. She walked across to a red covered chair and sat down in it.

"Haughty bitch, aint she?" said one of the ruffians in an aside to one of his compatriots, but in a voice loud enough for everyone to hear. Someone sniggered. Mrs. Mayhew blushed and put her handkerchief up to her mouth in the hope that it would stop people recognising her.

Another two people went into Court One before her. Eventually a male usher, wearing a black gown, came out of the door and called loudly, "Mrs. Mayhew and Miss Rose Ewing?" Mrs. Mayhew got to her feet and walked towards the door, her maid Rose following on quietly behind her. "Come with me, please," ordered the usher.

Mrs. Mayhew's confidence took a knock as she entered the courtroom. To her left were some wooden benches crowded with people. In front of her were the Police Inspector who was the Prosecutor and her defence lawyer, Mr. Baggins, of Baggins, Baggins and White, Solicitors. Mr. Baggins nodded towards her and gave her an encouraging smile as the usher indicated that both she and her servant should enter the dock together.

She went in first, with her servant following closely behind. Looking up, Mrs. Mayhew suddenly felt overawed at the sight of the three magistrates sitting above her on the bench. They were raised high enough to be looking down on them. Two of the magistrates were male, and the third was rather a demure looking woman whom she recognised as Mrs. Mountford, the wife of Colonel Mountford. She smiled towards her for now she felt as if she had at least found a kindred spirit. Above the three magistrates the Royal Coat of Arms was displayed proudly upon the wall, with its motto of "Dieu et mon Droit" in gold lettering below it. Mrs. Mayhew had enough learning to know that the motto translated into English as "God and my Right" but she was confident enough to think that she would soon be dismissed from the court.

The rather elderly man in the middle spoke. He had a military bearing and spoke crisply. "Good morning, Mrs. Mayhew, Miss Ewing. Please remain standing and listen carefully to the Clerk of the Court. He will ask you some questions which you must answer."

The court clerk stood to his feet. "You are Mrs. Gertrude Mayhew?"

"Of course!

"We have your address as being as The Oaks, The Park, Yeovil. Is that correct?"

"Yes!"

"And your date of birth is 1880?"

Someone in the court quietly chuckled but was instantly heard by the Chairman. "Silence!" he thundered. The noise instantly ceased.

Mrs. Mayhew coloured red, for she had always told her friends that she was just fifty years old. It was then that she noticed the reporter from the Western Gazette was busily scribbling down something in his notebook. "Oh my God!" she thought. "What will my friends think?" She answered the clerk with a simple, "Yes".

The clerk then addressed the servant. "And you are Miss Rose Ewing, a servant of Mrs. Mayhew."

The maid gave a little curtsey. "That is correct sir," she replied demurely.

"You also reside at The Oaks, The Park, Yeovil and you were born on the 11th September 1922. Is that correct?"

"Yes sir," she whispered.

"Thank you," replied the clerk.

The Clerk cleared his throat and took a sip of water before continuing. "Miss Ewing. You are charged under the 1940 Emergency Powers act that, on the 1st July 1942, you wasted food by causing half a loaf of bread to be put out for the birds. How do you both plead? Are you guilty or not guilty?"

Mr. Braggins stood to his feet. "If it pleases your honours, both ladies plead guilty to the offence as charged."

Mrs. Mayhew shouted, "That's ridiculous! The bread was stale and unfit for human consumption!"

"Silence!" ordered the chairman of the magistrates. He looked sternly towards the dock. "Sit down madam, and you Miss Ewing, if you will." The chairman of the bench then looked directly at the Prosecutor, a uniformed police inspector. "Inspector Wiltshire? What is your case, please?"

81

The inspector rose to his feet, carefully reading from a file placed before him. "If it pleases your worships, PC423 Gibbs was on foot patrol on the morning of Friday 3rd July 1942 at 0912 hours. As he was proceeding along The Park in Yeovil he saw the accused, Miss Rose Ewing, breaking up half a loaf of bread on to a large bird table. He approached the accused and cautioned her that she was committing the offence of wasting food. As he was speaking to her, the other accused, Mrs. Mayhew, came out and spoke sharply to the constable. She told him that the bread was stale and unfit for human consumption. That is why they were not eating it. He reminded Mrs. Mayhew of the offence that was being committed and invited the lady to take the bread back indoors for re-use."

The Chairman of the Bench frowned. "You mean to tell me that Mrs. Mayhew was given a chance to take the bread back inside?"

Mrs. Mayhew jumped to her feet. "This is ridiculous," she cried. "The bread was unfit to eat! It had gone mouldy!"

The Chairman glowered at her and Mrs. Mayhew sheepishly sat down. He turned his gaze back to the prosecuting policeman. "Carry on, Inspector," he ordered.

"Thank you, your honour." He coughed briefly and continued. "Mrs Mayhew refused point blank to take the food back inside. PC423 Gibbs then informed her that both she and Miss Ewing would be reported for the offence of wasting food." The police inspector closed the file. "That concludes the evidence for the prosecution, your honour. We ask for costs of One Guinea, if you please."

The Bench Chairman nodded. He looked at the defence solicitor. "Mr. Baggins. Have you anything to say?"

Mr. Baggins rose to his feet. "Your worships, Mrs. Mayhew is quite right in what she says. The bread was quite stale and unusable so she told her servant to feed it to the birds." The magistrates looked in sympathy towards the servant. "She felt that having the bread in the house constituted a health risk in that it would attract rats, and that is why she told her servant to break it up into crumbs for the birds."

The Chairman of the Bench looked at the female magistrate that sat on his left. He smiled at her and said, "Tell me, Mrs. Mountford, as you are the cook amongst us. What would you have done with the stale bread?"

Without hesitation, she stated, "Why, Mr. Chairman, I would have made you a nice bread pudding. You have tried some of my pudding, if you remember, when you came to supper at my house a few weeks ago, with your dear wife."

The Chairman nodded in appreciation. "Yes, and very nice it was too, my dear," he said approvingly, patting her hand. He removed the condescending smile from his face, having made his point clear, and spoke once again to Mr. Baggins. "Have you anything else to say?"

The solicitor wearily shook his head. "No, your worships," he admitted. He sat down, a look of defeat on his face.

The Chairman of the Bench spoke briefly to his two colleagues, wrote something down and showed it to them. They both nodded in agreement. Without looking at the defendants he said, "Stand up Mrs. Mayhew, Miss Ewing."

Both ladies rose to their feet. Mrs. Mayhew had a defiant look on her face. The police inspector smiled, confident that this particular chairman would deal harshly with the offence of food wasting.

The Chairman of the Bench held up the piece of paper before him and addressed the two ladies in the dock. "There is far too much food wasting going on in Yeovil and this court takes such matters very seriously." He looked directly at the servant girl. "Miss Ewing," he said. "The court takes the view that you were only doing what you had been ordered to do. Nevertheless," he continued sternly, "you should have drawn your employer's attention to the fact that the bread could have been used. We have taken this into consideration and fine you the sum of two shillings. You will not pay costs." The Chairman paused for a moment and said, "You may leave the dock."

The usher moved forward and opened the wooden door on the dock. It squealed slightly from an un-oiled hinge as it swung outwards. Miss Ewing, a grateful smile on her face, curtsied to the magistrates and quickly left the dock. The usher closed the door.

The Chairman of the Bench's face took on a stern vista. "As for you, Mrs. Mayhew, we take a very different view." He glanced sideways at his two colleagues and they gave him reassuring nods of support. "Not only did you waste valuable food, but you committed an offence by compelling your servant to place the stale bread out for the birds. Even when given the chance by the police constable to rectify your error, you refused to do so. We have considered sending you to prison for this offence."

Mrs. Mayhew gave an audible gasp, her hand flying to cover the crimson lips that were by now set in a pale face. Mr. Baggins instantly jumped to his feet. "Your Worships," he began to say.

The Chairman of the Bench waved him down. "Sit down Mr. Baggins and let me finish." He cleared his throat and took a sip of water. A little buzz went around the spectators in the courtroom and the reporter from the Western Gazette sat, pen poised, over his notebook. When he was satisfied that all was quiet the Chairman continued. "As I was saying; we did consider imprisonment but because of your previously impeccable character we have decided to impose a stiff fine instead." The Chairman paused for effect. "You will be fined the sum of Ten Guineas and pay the costs of One Guinea." He banged his gavel on the block in front of him. "Next case!" he ordered.

A humiliated and visibly shaken Mrs. Mayhew had to be helped from the dock by Mr. Baggins.

Historical note: In August 1940, a law was passed in Great Britain that made the wasting of food an imprisonable offence. Before the start of the war, Britain used to import approximately 55 million tons of food a year. The Germans actively attacked the merchant ships supplying this food as they saw that the lack of food would be an economic weapon.

To combat this reduction in food, one method introduced was that of rationing. Everyone had a ration book with a coupon in it for certain types of food. For example, one person's ration of tea per week was two ounces (two ounces of tea roughly equates to fifteen

84

of today's teabags). The shopper would purchase their allowance of two ounces of tea per person and the shopkeeper would remove the requisite number of coupons from the ration book.

Councils employed Food Inspectors to test the rationing system. One of the favourite tricks of these inspectors would be to ask for two ounces of tea. The shopkeeper would remove the coupon and then weigh up the loose tea (there were no tea bags in those days). The Food Inspector would then pretend to change their mind and ask the shopkeeper to make it four ounces of tea. Quite often, the harassed shopkeeper would forget to take out another two-ounce ration coupon. They would then be charged with breaking rationing restrictions.

In 1941, and under the Food Control Order, there were 2,300 prosecutions brought against shopkeepers for failing to strictly comply with the rationing systems. Of these prosecutions, there were 2,199 successful convictions. It is no small wonder that a Food Inspector was not the favourite person of the public. They were despised and loathed by everyone for the deliberate way they targeted small shops. At the time The General Secretary of the National Association of Outfitters declared that small traders "had become the most persecuted class in the whole of the country."

Cider and Bombs - 5th August, 1942.

On the 5th August 1942, after they had eaten dinner, Feldwebel Karl Blase and Unteroffizier Kurt Bressler walked purposefully and slowly around the still forms of their two Focke Wulfe 190 fighter aircraft. In the late evening's sun the dark shapes of the aeroplanes threw a menacing shadow across the tarmac runway. Both men considered that the aeroplanes before them were the finest fighter planes that the Reich had ever produced. Each of these powerful aircraft was armed with four 20mm cannons, as well as two machine guns that seemed to have been provided as an afterthought.

Beneath each camouflaged aircraft there hung a lethal 500-kilogram high explosive delayed action bomb. From the height at which they had instructed to attack their target this day, the use of ordinary bombs would have proved fatal to the two pilots.

"Well Kurt, it looks like we have a good evening for it, at least." The young sergeant pilot nodded in assent. He was never the one to say much. Karl Blase grimaced to himself, but at least he knew that Kurt would certainly be able to keep radio silence until they approached their target.

A deeply embedded spy had managed to relay back to Germany the exact position of the Nautilus Naval Weapons factory in Yeovil, a place the Germans had been seeking to locate for some time. He had even given them their aiming point. The target was to be found midway between the tower of St John's Church, in the very centre of the town of Yeovil, and St Michael's Church, which was just before the target. Thanks to a very helpful English road map the position of the factory had been exactly plotted.

The two pilots finished walking around their planes, and, each satisfied that everything was in order they climbed into their separate cockpits. Feldwebel Karl Blase started the powerful BMW radial engine of his aircraft, and giving a thumb up to his subordinate winger watched as Unteroffizier Kurt Bressler's engine also roared into life.

The routine order to take off was radioed to the pilots from the control tower of the captured airfield of Caen-Carpiquet, some six kilometres west of Caen. With the Feldwebel leading the way, the unteroffizier dutifully followed on behind. A bored staff officer came out of the control tower and lit a cigarette, idly watching the two aircraft as they zoomed up and away into the clear blue sky of the evening. Both planes did one circuit of the runway, making sure that everything was functioning correctly, and then they set course directly towards England.

Keeping low and skimming above the small waves at the ridiculous height of twenty feet, the two single wing fighter planes soon crossed over the Devon coast at Lyme Bay. The British defences were lackadaisical during that lovely summer's evening and they were not detected by the usually vigilant Royal Observer Corps. Hedge hopping, the two daring pilots then flew straight inland until they met the main Southern railway line. Banking right they followed it up towards Yeovil Junction station. If they had chanced to meet a train going in any direction, the two pilots had been directed to strafe them before moving on to their primary target.

As they passed over the main A37 road that went from Yeovil to Dorchester, a young lad excitedly jumped off his bike at Whistle Bridge. The aircraft were flying so low that he could clearly see the outline of both pilots. Cheerfully he waved towards the two low flying aircraft, mistakenly believing them to be British. Unteroffizier Bressler waved back, grinning to himself and enjoying the irony of the moment. That would make a lovely tale to narrate in the mess later that evening, and it would also earn him a few French brandies!

It was only then that the young lad saw the dark black crosses that adorned the wings of the aircraft. In a moment of unbridled horror, he suddenly realised that they were enemy fighters. Jumping on his bicycle he had the hopeless thought of cycling furiously to Yeovil Junction to warn them of the impending attack, but then he realised the futility of it all.

At Yeovil Junction station the railway officials were mightily relieved to see that the two fighter planes were not targeting them, at least not now. Both aircraft banked immediately to the right of the station and then banked hard once more, but this time to the left. They straightened out and flew in a straight line towards Babylon Hill.

A quick-thinking railway official swiftly telephoned the Royal Observer Corps headquarters in Yeovil, and within 20 seconds of receiving the call the air raid sirens wailed their urgent warnings across the sleepy Somerset town at approximately ten minutes past nine on that tranquil Sunday evening.

The man was sitting quietly on a rug by himself in a field above the main road that led to Sherborne, enjoying the balmy evening and sipping cider from a stone jug. From the top of Babylon Hill, he had secured himself an excellent view of Yeovil. He idly picked up his binoculars and surveyed the vista beneath him. Immediately to his front lay the bustling Yeovil Pen Mill station and its busy marshalling yards. The trains viewed from his position took on the size of toys as they shunted busily to and fro. Occasionally the station would be hidden from view as one of the freight trains carelessly blew smoke across the yard.

Ex-sergeant Charlie Shoesmith, formerly of the 2nd Battalion of the Royal Norfolk Regiment wiped his one good eye, for that was all he had. He had been badly wounded at the retreat from Dunkirk, fighting to the last with the rear-guard. An exploding shell had blown away most of his face, and it still showed. He had been given some sort of crude plastic surgery but he was so disfigured that even his own mother would not have known him. Not that she would have anyway, for Charlie was an orphan.

And that is precisely the reason why they had picked him. Having received a serious wound that day, Sturmbannfuhrer John Ellis, a British volunteer serving with the 14th Company, SS Division Totenkopf, had been hastily given a vital mission by his commander, Hauptsturmfuhrer Fritzknochlein. Although too badly wounded to serve as a fighting soldier anymore he could still carry out vital work for the Reich. He was to become a spy.

A British sergeant who bore a strikingly similar resemblance to him had been captured at the village of Le Paradis where the Royal Norfolk's had bravely resisted and temporarily halted the inexorable

German advance. After they had surrendered, all the remaining 97 survivors of the British battalion were immediately marched across the road from the farmhouse that they had so stoically defended. There they had been shot out of hand. The wounded sturmbannfuhrer had been given the dead sergeant's identity and uniform and his wounds dressed in British bandages.

From there he had been safely escorted back to Dunkirk, and as an act of "human kindness and German chivalry" he had been handed over to a British Aid Station and "allowed" to escape. Because of his wound, although not life threatening but none the less extremely serious, had been a head wound, the bogus sergeant had difficulty in talking correctly and had seemed to have lost his memory. That was his cover story and the stupid officials at the port of Weymouth, where he had been put ashore by his rescuers, had totally accepted it without question.

Mr Shoesmith peered with his one good eye through his binoculars towards the oil dump that lay invitingly before the railway station. It made a lovely target but he knew that it would never be so. He had been made aware of Churchill's and Stalin's personal agreement that Britain would never touch that oil, for this was Stalin's "personal oil dump". After the war, it would be sold in England at a high price, and the money sent to Stalin.

If the British kept to their end of the bargain the oil dump would not be bombed. Indeed, the Yeovil fuel dump formed an important part of Germany's invasion plans. When "Der Tag" eventually came Shoesmith would meet a group of German paratroopers and once more proudly don his infamous black uniform. He would then defend the oil dump with the paratroopers until the advancing German army reached them. What a prize that would be for the Reich! He licked his lips in anticipation.

He stood in front of a thick hedge that lay directly in front of a small wooded triangle of trees. Within that hedge there was a small radio transmitter that was tuned in to a very high frequency. He did not need to speak into it as the special detection equipment within the leading aircraft would lead them directly towards him. A wire aerial ran from the radio and up the side of an oak tree, the ivy hiding it from any casual inspection. He felt safe and secure in what he was doing.

The roar of two BMW radial engines approaching told him that the Fockwulfe's were on time and on target. Hastily he jumped to his feet, and snatching up the red and green chequered picnic blanket he had been sat on, ran out towards the middle of the field. Speedily he turned the blanket over and laid it lengthwise upon the ground. The underneath of the picnic blanket was completely white, with a red arrow painted upon it and pointing towards the target.

Feldwebel Karl Blase and Unteroffizier Kurt Bressler flew low over the top of the hill. "There!" shouted Kurt, a hint of excitement in his voice. "He is standing behind the white blanket with the arrow on it!"

"I have him on the radio receiver and can also see him," replied the Feldwebel. "We'll bank around again and fly straight over him."

Both aircraft turned to the right and headed towards Sherborne before finally banking to the left and headed straight for the distant church tower in Yeovil. As they flew over their man the Feldwebel wobbled his wings to show solidarity with the German agent. Charlie Shoesmith waved back ecstatically, happy to acknowledge the two aircraft as they flew breathtakingly close to him and headed in a straight line towards their target.

The leading Fockewulf 190 roared behind St Michael's church, tilting on its wingtip as it did so as it lined itself up with the further St John's church. A group of men and boy's playing cricket looked up as the both aircraft roared by, barely flying above the roofs of the houses. The noise emanating from the two aircraft was deafening and some of the boys clamped their hands over their ears to try and keep out the sound.

Feldwebel Karl Blase released his bomb, confident that it would hit its target. Suddenly he had to quickly take emergency avoiding action as belatedly some barrage balloons began to ascend in the morning air. Just for good measure he opened fire in the vain hope of hitting one.

The sinister dark bomb flew slowly forward in the air, rapidly losing height in its declining arc as it descended, hurtling low over the roof of the school at Grass Royal. At the same time Unteroffizier Kurt Bressler released his missive of death.

The first bomb clipped the roof of a house in a cul-de-sac known as Matthews Road and tumbled into its long back garden, its forward momentum bouncing it towards the houses in Gordon Road. The second bomb fell into Dampier Street and narrowly missed its target. With a thunderous roar both bombs exploded in quick succession, unleashing a hail of lethal shrapnel and a lung bursting pressure wave of air.

The aircraft roared over the centre of Yeovil, rapidly gaining height and coming perilously close to the tops of some large Elm trees that were growing at the top of Hendford Hill. As they did so, a light anti-aircraft gun belatedly fired, its tracers lazily arcing behind the second aircraft. By then it was much too late. Unteroffizier Kurt Bressler uncharacteristically gave a yell of delight over the intercom as both planes picked up the railway and gunned their engines to their fullest power as they headed back down towards Lyme Bay and safety. "If there be a God, let him give me a train!" he prayed fervently. Unfortunately for the unteroffizier, God was not listening that day.

Sergeant Browncie was playing skittles in the Great Western pub, his home side's alley. As ever he was dressed in his Home Guard uniform and his team of six was mostly made up of the other members of his little off-duty specialised unit. These men were men responsible for guarding the road that ran into and out of the Pen Mill Railway Station, a stone's throw away from the pub.

Their weapons were safely locked away in the unit's old van, parked outside the inn. Browncie went outside to sit on the wall and enjoy a fag with his cider when the air raid siren wailed its shrill warning. This time it was accompanied by the siren in Sherborne, indicating that something serious was about to happen. "Bugger "em!" thought Browncie. "It's probably another false alarm." At that precise moment, he heard the roar of the two aircraft as they descended over the hill and appeared to be flying directly towards him. Something else caught his eye too. Up on the crest of the hill he could see a man excitedly waving after the enemy aircraft, not the action of a friend.

Dropping his cider, he ran back inside to where his good friend and Home Guard N.C.O., Corporal Wally Preston, was getting himself another pint of cider at the bar.

"I hope that was our "planes?" he guessed.

"No, they be two girt German buggers and heading towards Westlands, I think." To prove his point, they suddenly heard the aircraft's bombs exploding and the pub's windows rattled noisily.

Browncie quickly summoned his Home Guard members of his skittles team around him. You could have heard a pin drop as the normally noisy pub went deathly quiet. "Listen up lads," said Browncie, a note of urgency in his voice. "I'm pretty certain that we have got ourselves a spy on top of Babylon Hill." The three members of the Home Guard exchanged glances with each other. "Now then, this be an order. Out to the van, quickly now! Load up your weapons, put a bullet up the spout and apply the safety catch. We may have to shoot!"

Rushing out to their parked vehicle the driver quickly unlocked the back door and swiftly handed the men their weapons. The magazines were already on the rifles, so all they had to do was pull back the bolts and let them go forward to insert a round into the firing chamber. When this was done Browncie said with authority, "Show me the safety catches on your guns!"

Each man proffered his loaded weapon towards the lieutenant, indicating that the safety catch on his weapon had been applied. "This is what we are going to do. Albert, when we get started drive over the River Yeo and turn left. As we approach the crossroads at Over Compton slow right down so we can all get out while you are still moving. You drive on over and keep going up to the church. Wait there for us. If you hear any shooting, drive back to Yeovil like the blazes and get reinforcements.

Now lads, when I say so we all get out of the moving vehicle and you form up behind me in single file. We be going to move along the road to the little copse that be there. The spy be just in the field on the other side of it. With any luck, we'll catch the bugger red handed!"

Charlie Shoesmith could not help himself as he whooped in exultation and punched his fist into the air in sheer joy as a secondary explosion occurred near the Nautilus factory. He could not see the building itself, for the smoke from the burning and damaged houses around it had entirely obscured his view. He was sure that the second bomb had hit the target, but he would have to wait until the smoke subsided before he radioed his report back to Berlin. His attention was wholly diverted to his task, the binoculars riveted on the spot where the factory should be. "A moment or two more, surely, and the smoke will clear!" he thought.

"Drop them glasses you Nazi bugger!" ordered a stern and bitter voice from somewhere behind him. Glancing over his shoulder he saw Sergeant Browncie and three men of the Home Guard. They were pointing their rifles at him.

Sturmbannfuhrer John Ellis of the 14th Company, S.S. Division Totenkopf, knew that he had been caught red-handed. He inwardly cursed himself for not being more aware. Luckily for him it was the inept and poorly trained Home Guard that had apprehended him. He had his back to the men, and knowing that he was far superior to them in combat, he slowly reached down for the loaded Luger pistol that he had stuffed in his waist band. Silently his hand grasped the pistol handle and gently he eased off the safety catch. He would not be hung as a spy. Spinning around he pointed his pistol at where the sergeant should have been and fired off two quick rounds before diving away to his right.

Browncie was not there, for he had moved. With a poacher's instinct, he knew that something bad was about to happen. He had moved two paces to his left after his challenge and had rapidly dropped down upon one knee. Browncie pulled the trigger on his rifle as quickly as he could. Five shots rang out.

With a look of utter surprise on his face, Sturmbannfuhrer John Ellis managed to fire one more shot into the air before he became another casualty of the second-world-war, but one whose true name would never be known. He staggered back a few steps before falling to the ground, stone dead.

"Bugger me!" said the corporal. "You've killed him Browncie!"

"I bloody well hope so! The bugger was going to try and pop us off!" From the hedge a little explosion took place. One of Shoesmith's shots had hit the radio, causing it to catch fire. The men of the Home Guard looked at it. "Quick!" said Browncie. "Put the fire out. We may need that as evidence."

In Gordon Road, one of the bombs had landed in the back gardens of three houses, numbers 13, 14 and 15. A huge crater, some 27 feet in diameter and going down to a depth of at least six feet, now commanded the scene. A broken water pipe slowly began to flood it. When the bomb exploded, 46-year-old Albert Hussey had been busily feeding his rabbits, a source of wartime food. He was hit in the head by shrapnel and sadly would die the next day.

38-year-old Albert George Mitchell, a member of the Royal Observer Corps, was at home digging his back garden at Number 8, Grass Royal. His father in law was helping him, cursing roundly as he pulled out a root of Bindweed. Flying fragments of shrapnel from the same bomb that killed Albert Hussey also killed George Mitchell, but instantly. His father in law, standing nearby, managed to escape with a few cuts and bruises. He looked on in a horrified silence at the sight of the gaping head wound that had killed his popular son-in-law. He gave a moan of comprehension when he realised the shock his darling daughter was in for. In total, two houses in Gordon Road had been demolished whilst many others were badly damaged.

In nearby Dampier Street, the second bomb had done far more material damage. 60-year-old Elsie Farwell of Number 6, Dampier Street, had also been mortally wounded and was fated to die the next day. In addition, eight houses were destroyed, and eighteen more lay badly damaged. The target, the Nautilus factory which made compasses for the Royal Navy, received minor damage but could function normally.

From St Michaels Road in Yeovil the Polish Ambulance Brigade stationed in the hall next to the church hastily mobilised. Bells clanging urgently, they quickly made their way to the scene of devastation. Calmly and professionally they moved amongst the injured, carrying out triage and gently removing the dead and wounded. The casualties were quickly transported to Yeovil's hospital. At nine forty p.m., the sirens sounded the "All Clear". This was the last occasion that Yeovil would be bombed during the second-world-war.

LEST WE FORGET

HUSSEY, Albert Victor, Home Guard.
MITCHELL, Albert George, Royal Observer Corps.
FARWELL, Elsie, civilian.

Bibliography:

1. "Ron Batty, WW2 People's War"

The Burning Bomber - 23rd January, 1943.

The Vickers manufactured Wellington Bomber MkIc, serial number R1799, of Number 15 Operational Training Unit waited patiently on the main runway at R.A.F. Harwell in Berkshire, its Bristol Hercules twin engines humming at a steady and controlled rate.

The pilot took a curious comfort from knowing that the geodesic duralumin framework of the fuselage of the aircraft gave it the ability to absorb tremendous punishment, allowing it to keep flying where other aircraft would have dropped out of the sky. This criss-cross of alloy channel beams had wooden battens screwed into the metal on which a dope fabric skin was stretched and held into place by more screws.

The aircraft bore freshly painted camouflage markings, the heady smell of which permeated the aircraft and reminded one of a paint shop. Try as he might, Pilot Officer Lean, the navigator, could not avoid that smell which had made him physically gag a couple of times.

A green light was flashed from the control tower by a shaded torch, indicating that the aircraft now had permission to take off. Sgt Nichols gradually increased the throttle and fed more power to the engines. The aircraft shuddered as it fought to overcome its brakes, and then Nicholls let her go. The lights of the runway blinked on, illuminating the edges of the stretch of tarmac the bomber had to use. The cumbersome aeroplane lumbered forward between the masked lights and, on reaching take off speed, despite its bulk, soared gracefully up into the night sky of the 23rd January, 1943.

This was no operational sortie, but merely an evening navigation exercise to the Royal Naval Air Station down there in Somerset. The crew thought of it as a milk run. Nevertheless, the machine guns in the front and tail turrets were fully armed, for one never knew if a marauding German night fighter might suddenly pounce on them. Even at this stage of the war vigilance was vital to survival.

The crew of the aircraft normally consisted of 6 men, but for tonight's exercise there were only 5 of them on the flight.

After the aircraft had been airborne for a few minutes the voice of Sergeant Leigh-Morgan in the rear turret spoke calmly through the intercom system. "Can I test fire my gun's skipper?"

Nicholls smiled. L.M., as he was nicknamed, was usually the first to call in. "Both turrets, 3 second burst to test guns," he said, speaking confidently into the microphone attached to his throat. The aircraft shuddered as the nose and rear guns fired almost as one. Tracer from the front guns streaked up towards the heavens and quickly lost their red colouring as they arched away. The smell of gun smoke rapidly filled the aircraft. Nicholls gave a boyish grin. The testing of the guns always hyped him up for any mission, whether it was for real or just a training jaunt. This was going to be an easy flight.

It was just about 6.45 p.m. and Corporal Alfred Duke of the Home Guard got on his bicycle. He had been on duty in one of the pillboxes by Speckington Lane that his unit was responsible for, and over on the far side of the Royal Naval airfield. His group were also in charge of checking people in and out of Speckington Manor, the big commandeered farm house that lay at the end of the blind lane that led up to it. Duke didn't know what went on in there, except he knew that radio masts seemed to be poking out everywhere from the place.

He lived at the nearby village of Limington and it would take him about twenty minutes to get himself home in the darkness. He knew the roads around the airfield like the back of his hand. There was no need for a shielded light anyway, for the brightness of the stars illuminated the road for him.

The airfield was in complete darkness as he cycled along the lane and he knew that there would be no flying of aircraft tonight. In the distance, he heard the unmistakeable sound of a heavy engine aircraft heading towards him. He stopped and listened intently. "Hmph! Wellington!" he thought to himself, testing his own recognition skills.

At 6.45 p.m., the starboard engine of aircraft R1799 suddenly began to go wrong. The noise changed from a smooth running one and it began to run roughly. There was a sudden back firing of the engine causing Nicholls and Lean to exchange anxious glances.

"We're about 2 minutes away from the Yeovilton circuit by my reckoning," said Lean. Nicholls nodded his head, grateful for his Navigator's confirmation.

He pressed the intercom switch to contact his RT man, Smiler Miles. "Smiler, get on to Yeovilton and tell them we are having a problem with our starboard engine will you."

"Will do skipper," came the prompt reply.

The misfiring engine suddenly began to race and the aircraft started to slew violently to port, losing height as it did so. "Christ!" called Nicholls. Beads of sweat formed on his forehead as he fought to control the aircraft, and as suddenly as it had begun the engine returned to normal as he almost overcorrected his counter manoeuvre. Just as suddenly the faulty engine began to race again and once more began its unauthorised turn to port.

"Bugger this!" called Nicholls into the intercom. "Put out a Mayday, Smiler. We are going to have to land her."

The Radio Operator replied in a cool, laconic tone, "Transmitting now."

The engine suddenly returned to normal, and then the revolutions dropped, this time forcing it around to port. "Where's the airfield now, Slim?" he said tersely to his navigator.

Lean pointed a little to the left. In the distance a small Aldis lamp winked at them and indicated the beginning of the runway.

"Smiler, any reply?"

"It's just coming through now, skipper. Clear to land on runway marked by the Aldis Lamp."

Nicholls spoke into his microphone. "All crew, we are making an emergency landing at Yeovilton." Laconically he stated the obvious. "For those of you who have not noticed, the starboard engine is playing up! Everyone buckle themselves in please. It might be a rough ride!" He smiled as he heard some ironic cheers coming over the intercom.

Corporal Duke had made his way along the main B.3151, locally known as Heathcote Road, and vigorously cycled into Bineham Lane. This narrow road led directly into Yeovilton Village, and then on over the river bridge to Limington, where he lived. The lane was bounded on its right by the River Yeo with the airfield away to its left. The high hedge had recently been cut right down so that any low flying aircraft could easily clear it. A couple of times before that the hedge had been clipped by trainee naval pilots and a few accidents had occurred, luckily none of them fatal. Albert got off his bicycle and listened intently as he heard the struggling bomber flying towards him, looking towards the direction where the it was coming from.

It was too far over to the left of the runway to land, and it would have to go around again. In support of his thoughts a red Verey's light suddenly ignited in the air, warning the pilot that he had got it wrong.

The noise from the aircraft became louder and louder, and suddenly out of the blackness it roared over his head at about 200 feet, its starboard engine screaming in protest. Something hot and wet hit Albert on the cheek, and putting his hand up he felt a splatter of engine oil. He tasted it to make sure. "That poor bugger is in trouble!" he said aloud.

Nicholls was worried. He was losing height fast and finding it difficult to stop the aircraft yawing all over the place. He had thought of making height and ordering the crew to bail out. He would then attempt to bring in the aircraft on his own.

Unfortunately, the aircraft would not respond to his demand for it to climb. Instead it flew lower and lower and was almost uncontrollable. He now knew that he was really faced with no option, he would have to crash land it.

Keeping his voice as calm as possible he said, "Crash landing positions everyone." The wheels of the aircraft were already down and he made his approach, this time anticipating the sudden surge in engine power. He had learned by the engine noise just about when this was going to occur. When it did, he was ready. Gripping the column firmly he fought against the yaw and managed to keep it steady. He grinned in satisfaction as the Aldis Light flashed green at him and the landing lights of the airfield were suddenly switched on. He glanced at his Navigator and smiled. Lean gave him the thumbs up. At about 20 feet above the runway and with no room for error, the starboard engine suddenly blew up.

Duke looked on in horror as the approaching aircraft suddenly lost control after the explosion, the port engine pushing it towards starboard. The bomber seemed to turn directly sideways on to him and gracefully completed a circle before hitting the ground and sliding through the newly cut hedge and across Bineham Lane. At 1905 hours, the doomed aircraft crashed into the River Yeo and spectacularly burst into flames.

"Bloody hell!" he shouted to no-one. The crash had occurred no more than a hundred yards away from him. Cycling furiously, he headed towards the scene of the disaster. Jumping off his bike he threw it against the hedge and as an afterthought removed the .303 rifle strapped to his back and placed it upon the bike. He ran pell-mell towards the burning 'plane. Duke was within 30 yards of it when it violently exploded, throwing him physically to the ground and knocking the senses out of him. When he recovered, he found that he was on his hands and knees and somehow crawling away from the aircraft.

Shaking his head, he forced himself to his feet. From the burning bomber, he could hear horrendous screaming. He forced himself towards the blazing aircraft, holding his hand in front of his eyes, trying to see where the screaming was coming from. What he saw chilled him to the bone, despite the heat.

Struggling to get out of the rear turret the gunner could clearly be seen silhouetted against the dancing flames that raged inside the aircraft. He was trying to get out. Duke was an old soldier and had seen battle before. He did not let the flames put him off and managed to make his way along the outside fuselage of the burning aircraft. The rear gunner was banging desperately at the Perspex, trying in vain to escape. It was jammed against a willow tree. Duke grabbed the gun barrels of the machine gun with his bare hands and cried out in pain as they were badly burnt. Nevertheless, he tried desperately to swing the turret around for the trapped airman to escape.

He heard two vehicles stop close by, and in a moment he was joined by a Royal Naval Warrant Officer in uniform and a local farmer, Mr Elford, whom he knew slightly. Both newcomers ignored the potential peril of the aircraft blowing up and rushed to Duke's aid.

The extra strength of the two men paid the dividend they were hoping for and the turret swung around, exposing the burning airman. Reaching into the turret, Duke pulled the airman's legs out, dragging off one of the airman's burning rubber boots as he did so, again searing his already burnt hands. He did not seem to feel it.

"You two grab his legs!" he shouted to his two companions. "He is still strapped to his seat!" Coolly Duke reached inside and undid the restraining straps that held the trapped airman a prisoner of the raging inferno that was the aircraft. Suddenly the airman was free and they dragged him away from the aircraft, but as they did so there was another explosion which hurled them all to the ground. Duke threw himself over the rescued airmen to protect him, and then all three men got up and, stumbling and cursing, successfully carried the badly burnt rear gunner away to a safe distance. The clanging of bells announced the arrival of two ambulances and three fire engines.

Placing the injured airman down in the road, Duke ran back to the burning aircraft. One glance told him that there was nothing else that he could do. The remainder of the crew had been consumed by the fire and were all dead. Sadly, he shook his head and made his way back to the road.

A naval officer had arrived and taken charge of the situation. Duke, seeing that he could do no more, picked up his discarded rifle and sat astride his bicycle. He cycled the two miles to his local pub, the Lamb and Lion at Limington, grateful for the cool air that passed over his body. On arrival, he got off his bicycle and propped it against the stone wall of the village inn. A couple of the locals looked at him curiously, for they could see the flames from the downed aircraft from where they were.

"Evening Fred," said the landlord. "You are looking a bit dishevelled, my lad."

"Feel it too," he replied. The landlord poured out a pint of cider into Duke's stone cider glass and passed it across to him. Fred picked it up and took a grateful gulp of the cool, clear liquid.

"Christ Fred!" exclaimed the landlord. "What the bloody hell has happened to your hands?"

It was then that the adrenalin wore off and Corporal Duke of the Home Guard looked on in astonishment at the state of his burnt hands. Suddenly he felt the sheer agony of his wounds. "I think that you had better get me an ambulance," he grumbled, wincing in pain. As an afterthought, he said, "But not before I finish me cider!"

LEST WE FORGET

677751 Sergeant (Pilot) Alan George Holroyd NICHOLS, aged 28.
131903 Pilot Officer (Navigator) Geoffrey William LEAN, aged 30.
1335238 Sergeant (Air Bomber) Donald William MILES, aged 20.
1131409 Sergeant (Air Gunner) Padraig De Valera McMAHON, age unknown.

In grateful thanks for his service:

Sergeant (Air Gunner) P.R. LEIGH-MORGAN.

In grateful thanks for their bravery and the saving of the life of Sergeant P.R. LEIGH-MORGAN

Corporal Frederick Alfred DUKE British Empire Medal,
(he was awarded this honour for his part in the rescue).
Warrant Officer Writer H.R. BARTHOLOMEW R.N.
Mr E.C. ELFORD, Farmer.

The Price of Oil - 1st September, 1943.

It was a seemingly normal beginning to a warm summer's day in Yeovil. Browncie snorted and reluctantly emerged from his cider induced sleep. He knew it was morning because he had no curtains on the window. As soon as the dawn had broken the rising sun had forcefully stabbed unwanted shafts of sunlight into his eyes, dragging him back into the land of the living. Well, that was except that Mrs Jenning's bloody cockerel next door had started to crow just before dawn and had greatly disturbed him. He'd promised himself to fix that bugger one day. But today was not to be the day. His head ached far too much to bother with such a mundane but pleasurable expectation.

He yawned and allowed himself a wide and luxurious stretch, groaning as his body moved a little too quickly. His aching back immediately reminded him that this was why he was not in the regular armed forces. Instead he found himself as a captain in the Home Guard, but a very special captain indeed.

On reflection, he was content to allow himself an extravagantly loud burp. This he gratefully managed without spilling any of his stomach's contents. This act seemed to have upset his equilibrium because at the same time it also caused him to loudly break wind. Sighing, he pulled the huge duck feather eiderdown firmly over his head, hoping to get another hour's sleep or two in the warmth of the downy embrace. He immediately surfaced, his lungs gratefully gulping in large dollops of what passed as fresh air in the small cottage that he rented. His recalled that his manful attempt to drink the Royal Marine pub dry of Scrumpy on the previous Saturday night had failed abysmally. His distended stomach reminded him of how much cider he had consumed. "Christ!" he thought. "I'm getting better! Must have put away at least fifteen pints last night!"

On the other side of the bed a hidden lump rolled like a wave breaking quietly on the pebble shoreline at Bridport. It muttered through sleepy lips; "You stinking bastard". She then turned her back on Browncie, displaying an invitingly warm rump that now faced provocatively upwards towards her husband. Browncie glanced at his wife and wrinkled up his nose as she too gently broke wind. He playfully gave her bottom a loving smack with the open palm of his hand. The smell of his and her body aromas mingled together and floated around the still air of the small bedroom, almost creating a green hue in the air above the bed. "Bugger it!" he grumbled, looking lecherously at his wife. He decided that the normal rumpty-tumpty he usually had in the morning would not take place. Well, not just yet anyway!

His left hand scratched his head as his right hand wandered down to gently scratch a rarely washed crotch. Browncie gave a large yawn before he brought his hand up and gave it a sniff. Coupled with the smell of the previous night's cider it made him retch. Swiftly he sat up. He needed a crap!

Captain Browncie made his way down the steep, rickety wooden stairs of the pair of houses. They were known locally as the Pen Mill Cottages and had once been a public house known as the Old Pen Mill Inn. Located almost opposite the town's mill itself, the inn had been purchased by the Great Western Railway for its workers and was now a two up and two down. Unusually the inner porch was a common one with the house next door. You entered through the front door and either took the door to the left or to the right. He lived behind the right-hand door along with his wife and son of three. There was also a common stairway that both families used. This stairway led to a small balcony with a door on either side. Again, Browncie's room was that one on the right.

One evening he had come back from the Great Western pub far too inebriated to worry much about it. He recalled that it had been a dark and stormy winter's night. When he had staggered in, tripping noisily over the large white cat that belonged to no-one but habitually frequented the place, he found that his wife had already gone to bed. He lurched clumsily up the stairs and had fallen over on the top step, disorienting himself. As quietly as any drunk does he entered his room, throwing off his clothes and chuckling softly to himself as he did so. Browncie had leapt naked into bed, full of good intentions. He remembered snuggling up to his wife and thinking that she had lost weight. He gently fondled her breasts and

104

randomly thought that they felt tight. Dropping his hand between his wife's thighs he suddenly encountered a thick hairy bush that she did not have! He sat bolt upright, a moment of sobriety entering his head.

Mrs Jennings screamed loudly and jumped out of bed. The hasty striking of a match caused a half-burnt candle to suddenly ignite into flame. The lady looked at him, horror etched plainly on her face. Browncie frowned. "Bloody hell!" he gave as what passed as an apology to him. "Sorry missus. I've got the wrong bloody room!" He leapt out of Mrs Jennings matrimonial bed and quickly grabbing his discarded clothing, beat a hasty retreat to where his snoring wife slept the sleep of the dead. He also gave a thankful prayer that Mrs Jenning's big husband, Tom, the former ganger on the Great Western Railway, was not there. The poor man had recently been called up and just as quickly had been posted as missing believed dead.

Captain Browncie gratefully opened the heavy oak back door and made his way gingerly down to the privy at the bottom of the garden. A sudden twist in his stomach meant that he increased the speed of his gait. He frowned as he began to worry if he could make it. Lifting his night shirt, he threw open the door to the privy, its ever-present stench welcoming him to the glory of the sunny morning. Gratefully he slumped down on the wooden seat and immediately relieved himself. Its cider aroma inexorably masked the stench of what had been fermenting beneath him in the ground.

As he looked up he realised that there was no newspaper on the nail behind the door to wipe his bottom dry. "Bugger!" he thought. He groaned a little as about another two pints of what smelt like neat cider left his body, splashing noisily against the dirt wall of the privy some three feet beneath him. He put his hand down to wipe himself as clean as he could. "Bloody war!" he muttered out loud.

As if to remind him that there was a war on, the air raid warning siren began its characteristic low winding howl, rising to the wail of a banshee. It didn't bother him as lately the air raid sirens had always been false alarms. 1943 was proving to be a quiet year.

Anyway, he reasoned, if an attack did come they would be far more interested in the nearby Royal Naval Air Station at Yeovilton, or perhaps the Westland Aircraft factory in Yeovil itself. No, he had no need to worry. He continued sitting there for a moment or two before reluctantly rising from his boxed wooden toilet. As if to prove he was right, the "All Clear" sounded almost immediately. "Stupid sods!" thought Browncie. "Those Observer Corps twats must have identified one of our aircraft as an enemy fighter again! Pah!"

He walked back up the shared garden path towards the rear entrance of his cottage, briefly stopping at the iron water pump and the pool of water in the stone trough that it held beneath it. Lifting his nightshirt, he started to wash his soiled bottom. Every so often he sniffed his hand to check if it was clean.

"You dirty sod!" called an irate Mrs Jennings. She too had been visiting her privy and was walking back up the garden over the well-trodden earth. She had to pass right by him. "Why can't you have a bowl and wash indoors like any decent man would do?"

Lifting his nightshirt fully up to expose his complete body from the chest down, Browncie leered, "What's the matter my dear. Like some of it?"

Mrs Jennings gave a little squeal and averted her eyes, running up the garden towards the safety of her house. "And you've got a fat ass!" Browncie called triumphantly after her. The Cockerel crowed twice. "Shut up, you sod!" he called.

Browncie really held his rank and privileges at the behest of the Prime Minister of the time, Winston S. Churchill. Why? Browncie never really knew for sure. All he was certain of was that he had received a personal letter from him promoting him to the rank of a captain in the Home Guard, and a captain responsible only to the Prime Minister himself. It also congratulated him on the dispatch of "a despicable German spy". On completion of reading the letter, and if he wished to accept his commission, Captain Browncie was to keep the oil dump safe, it was not to be used by anyone. The letter he held was his authority.

Browncie did what the Prime Minister ordered without any thought of the consequences. He had been made a captain for God's sake! Not only that, he was to report to Churchill himself if anyone attempted to take the oil. No one would ever know that, of course. And for this acknowledgement by the great man, what did he have to do?

It was quite simple really. Behind Pen Mill Cottages, where he lived, an oil dump had suddenly appeared. It was owned by the Russian Oil Producers and, unbeknown to him, under the direct control of Joseph Stalin himself. Somewhere along the line the Prime Minister of Great Britain and Northern Ireland, Winston S. Churchill had made a secret deal with Stalin to spare this stock of high quality, expensive oil. The captain in the Home Guard had calculated that at a modest estimate over a million gallons of the stuff was stored there.

All Browncie had to do was to open the special security lock that sealed the main gates and patrol around inside of the compound each day. There were several large white sided buildings with galvanised roofing. Each building had a large door that was secured by a huge padlock. His duty was to check that the padlocks had not been tampered with. The remaining space inside the square was taken up with forty-five-gallon steel drums filled with engine oil. The whole compound was surrounded by a high galvanised fence, each part of the top of the fence being fashioned into a razor-sharp point. To try and climb over the fence would have meant life threatening injuries.

And what did he receive for the performance of this service? Well, Browncie carried out his duties as a captain in the Home Guard quite seriously, particularly as Churchill had ordered him to do so. Apart from that, the cheque that he regularly received from the Russian Oil Producers at two pounds a month to cover his "expenses" helped him to be more than vigilant. Browncie wandered off to do his duty at the oil depot.

He was whistling a tuneless air when he approached the fuel dump, its camouflaged huts and netting rejecting the rays of the warm morning sun and showing no reflections. Browncie gave a blissful smile as his head ache was starting to subside. Looking down at his keys he was unaware of a man waiting behind the hedge on his left.

"Browncie!" a voice called urgently.

The captain stopped and looked towards the hedge. "Who the bloody hell's that?"

"It be me, Tom Ricketts."

"What the bloody hell be you doing hiding behind the hedge, Tom?"

"Waiting for thee, of course."

Browncie stopped at the main gate of the oil depot. He fiddled with his keys before inserting the correct one in the huge main gate padlock. "Come on out where I can see thee, you bugger. What do you want?" The captain pushed the gate open, his mind full of suspicion.

Tom Ricketts pulled his eighteen-stone body weight over the five-barred wooden gate. He jumped off the bottom rung with all the grace of a bull elephant falling from twenty feet. He staggered over the uneven grass in front of the gate and for a minute Browncie thought that the little man of barely five feet in height was going to fall flat on his face. Ricketts was puffing a little. "Have you got any oil?"

Browncie gave Tom a disdainful look. Opening his arms in an expansive gesture he pointed towards some of the now visible huge barrels of oil that lay neatly stacked within the compound. "Don't be bloody stupid!" he said.

"No! I baint being bloody stupid at all, Browncie. I know you got plenty of oil in here, I can see it. No. What I means is, 'ave you got any of it to spare like?"

"It isn't mine, it's the government's."

Tom Ricketts gave an expansive wink with his right eye and the index finger of his right hand tapped his nose. "No. I mean, have you got any that you could see your way to selling me?"

Captain Browncie, Home Guard, pulled himself up to his five foot eleven inches. Throwing his chest out he said, "What sort of man do you take me to be, Tom Ricketts!"

A horrified look appeared on Tom's face. "A thoroughly honest one, captain!" he said.

"That be right, and don't you bloody well forget it!"

Browncie walked through the gate of the oil compound. Tom Ricketts eyes bulged at the sight of all the oil barrels stacked neatly end on end and reaching up to ten barrels high.

"Christ almighty! How much of it have you got here?"

Browncie turned on the man. "You bloody well mind your own business about that, Tom. That's for me to know and for you to find out!"

"Blimey, Browncie. Nobody is going to miss a few gallons of it now, are they?"

"What the bloody hell do you mean?"

Tom Ricketts looked about him, making sure that no-one was nearby listening. He gave his head a scratch and a crafty look came upon his face. "I know someone who will give you two bob a gallon for that engine oil."

Browncie quickly did a swift calculation in his head. Each oil drum contained 45 gallons of pure engine oil. At two shillings to the gallon it meant that each whole barrel was worth the grand sum of ninety shillings to him, which was four pounds ten shillings! He hastily turned his face away from Tom Ricketts because he did not want him to see the look in his eyes. The sum offered was over a month's wages for one measly little barrel.

Tom waited a moment or so. "Well, what do you reckon?"

Browncie sighed. For a moment or so he had been sorely tempted, for he was not a rich man. "No, I don't think so Tom. Now you go away and I'll pretend that you never spoke to me."

Tom Ricketts stood his ground. "I said to the man who asked me to talk to you that you would not settle for two bob a gallon." Tom hesitated for a moment and said, "What if he was to offer you half a crown a gallon instead?"

"Half a crown a gallon?"

"Yes, half a crown a gallon."

Browncie paused. "How much does he want?"

"As much as you can give him."

"How do I know I can trust you?"

Tom Ricketts smiled. "You know I took Maggie Jennings out a few times, don't you?" Browncie shook his head in a negative fashion, for he did not know that his neighbour had been seeing anyone. "Well, I have. I've 'ad her you know, a few times, and a bloody good little rattle she is too!"

Browncie opened his arms in an expansive manner. "So, what the bloody hell has that got to do with me?"

Tom Ricketts smiled an evil smile. "Your missus doesn't know that you jumped into bed with her, does she?"

Browncie put his face close to that of Toms and snarled, "You trying to blackmail me, you bugger?"

Tom Ricketts quickly stood back a pace. "No, no!" he said. "It's completely the opposite. I tell you that because it shows you that I can keep a secret, and a secret it will remain Browncie, whatever the outcome of our little deal."

Browncie nodded, feeling a little trapped. He smiled. "In that case Tom, I'm sure we can work something out."

"Good! I felt sure that we could arrive at some sort of arrangement."

"I'd want the money up front though."

"No problem. When can I have some, then?"

Three nights later Browncie went to the outside toilets of the Royal Marine Public House. Tom Ricketts followed him shortly afterwards and quietly passed him an envelope. In it was five pounds twelve shillings and sixpence, a veritable fortune to him. An hour later Browncie sauntered down to do a night time check of his oil depot. He rolled a barrel of oil outside the compound and silently stood there, slightly agitated as he awaited the illegal transfer. He felt apprehensive about the whole deal, but he knew that no-one would question him.

A small covered lorry with no lights quietly approached him. The lorry stopped and Tom Ricketts and somebody else jumped out of the vehicle's cab. Swiftly they dropped the tailboard and two planks were hastily pulled out. Tying a rope around the barrel they rolled it up the planks, keeping the rope tight as they did so to ensure that the barrel did not run back. The whole transaction was over in less than a minute. Quickly the tailboard of the lorry was pulled up and the vehicle was gone. Browncie saw it moving away and heard the vehicle chug up the steep A.30 road as it passed over Babylon Hill. He smiled to himself. Tomorrow the oil drum would probably be in London and its contents had probably already been sold.

This happened about once a month for the next six months. Browncie had, for the first time in his life, some spare money. He also had a bloody good time in the pub each night. But now he had also lost seven barrels of oil and he felt as if he could no longer cover the losses up. He had to devise a plan to hide his indiscretions.

"That's your lot Tom," he said, rolling out the last barrel. "I can't cover me tracks if I gives you any more of this oil."

Ricketts nodded in understanding. "I thought that there would come a time," he said.

Browncie nodded his head in agreement. "I'm afraid that now is that time, Tom. This has to be your last barrel."

Tom wrapped his arm around Browncie's shoulders in a friendly fashion. "Come with me," he said. "I think that we can solve this problem quite easily."

The two men walked away from the now familiar truck while the man in it secured his ill begotten load. It was not for him to listen to the plans of the two men. After Tom was certain he was out of earshot he came up with his plan.

"We do it in one job lot," he explained. "Next time I'll take 250 barrels!"

"What! No bloody way!" said Browncie sharply.

"Hang on a minute, listen to what I have to say."

"Not bloody likely. Taking that much will get me – and you – both hanged!"

Tom Ricketts gave one of his peculiar laughs. "Not bloody likely, my boy. I have some contacts in London that will prove very useful to us."

Browncie's brow furrowed. "Bloody London! I thought that was where you were taking my oil!"

Tom gave a grin, the whiteness of his teeth gleaming in the darkness. "But they be bloody good men," he said. "They know the price of oil."

"I bet they bloody do!"

"Look, me old mucker. Don't you worry about it. For 250 barrels, I'll give you £1,250 in cash, in your hand, the night before the move."

Browncie started in surprise. "£1,250?"

"Yea, £1,250, all in crisp one pound notes.

"£1,250?"

Tom smiled. "That's what I said."

Browncie rubbed his chin thoughtfully. That sum would be enough to buy the house of his dreams and still have plenty left over. It would set him up for life. He paused thoughtfully and then shook his head. "If I thought for a moment we could get away with it, I would."

"Ah!" said Ricketts. "But you can!"

"How can I?"

Tom once again draped his arm around Browncie's shoulders. "It's so bloody simple, me old mate. I've told you, I've got contacts. I can arrange for plenty of army Lorries to be here to collect the oil. Once we got 'em loaded, we'll be gone, never to return."

"But what about them army boys? One of them is sure to smell a rat."

Tom Ricketts gave a little chuckle. "You don't think that they'll be real army Lorries, or real army soldiers, do you?"

Browncie grinned. "You mean, they'll be your men?"

He smirked. "Now you got it."

The Captain nodded in understanding. "Alright, that covers that question."

"How about if I give you a written order from Winston S. Churchill himself to release 350 barrels of oil to Captain John Williams, Royal Engineers. Would you release it to him?"

Browncie was shocked. "How do you know about me and Churchill?"

"Walls talk, you know." Tom Ricketts kept his own counsel for a moment or so before saying, "Well? Would you?"

"Would I do what?"

"Release the oil if ordered to?"

There was no hesitation on Browncie's behalf. "Of course I bloody would!"

"Well then. I have a man in London who can write Churchill's signature so well that even Churchill would think it was his own!"

Browncie shook his head in disbelief. He nodded in agreement before saying sharply, "You said you only wanted 250 barrels."

"That's right. We leave another 50 here so I can come and buy 'em off you in the future, and the other 50 would cover what we have already taken and leave some barrels for you to dispose of privately, if you see what I mean."

"But what if someone from the Russian Oil Company comes to count the barrels?"

"Well, you'll have Churchill's letter, don't you?"

Captain Browncie grinned happily. He was about to become a rich man and even have a little income to come for another year or so. As far as he could see the plan was fool proof. Two weeks later he happily accepted the usual brown envelope, although this time it was a larger envelope and stuffed with £1,250 in pound notes.

The collection of the oil drums took place before dawn. There was nothing unusual about army convoys travelling the roads, and whatever they carried they would not be stopped by the civilian police. There was a risk of being stopped by military police but even that eventuality had been covered. John Williams, a fine actor, would be wearing the uniform of a Guard's captain, and he would also be wearing the ribbon of the Victoria Cross. As a back-up to the plan, he had a forged letter from the Prime Minister, Winston Churchill, to state that the convoy was on a most secret mission and it was not to be hindered. Tom Ricketts was dressed as an army sergeant. He was the driver of the lead vehicle in which the captain rode as a passenger.

11,250 gallons of the finest engine oil drove away from the Russian Oil Company's store in Yeovil before four o'clock that morning. The convoy followed the meandering A.30 main road without any trouble and by five thirty a.m. they were approaching Salisbury, ready to pass though the army garrison town before too many people were about.

As they approached the outskirts of Salisbury, and despite the orders to keep apart at hundred feet, the convoy was almost nose to nose as they meandered through the streets of Wilton. It was here that they came across an overturned vehicle from an earlier accident that forced them to come to a grinding halt. The trucks were sat there, engines idling and with a fuming Captain Williams berating some Pioneer Corps soldiers to clear the road when total disaster struck.

Two patrolling Fockewulf 190 fighters, their ammunition and bomb racks full, came across the halted vehicles. The two German pilots, with Feldwebel Horst Kirsh as the lead pilot, could not believe their luck and, in line astern, raked the convoy with 30 mm cannon fire before turning to look at their handiwork. The dark smoke belching from the Lorries told Kirsh that whatever cargo the vehicles carried was important. "Bombs, Willie!" he ordered. Once more the enemy aircraft came screaming back into their unhindered attack, dropping their 500-kilogram fragmentation bombs.

When the aircraft left, every single truck was burning brightly with palls of black smoke covering everything around it. Browncie never did sell the extra drums of oil and he never did see Tom Ricketts again.

Historical note: There really was an oil dump belonging to the Russians in Yeovil during that time. Nobody appears to know what eventually became of it after the war. No-one knows what happened to Captain Browncie either, for he, too, mysteriously disappeared.

The Lost Love- 30th March, 1944.

"Private Russo, sir!" barked the American First Sergeant, one of the more senior Engineer Non-Commissioned Officers of the unit. Russo marched into his Company Commander's office and saluted. The American captain was studying a folder and returned the salute in a casual manner. He read most of the page before putting the folder down flat on the wooden desk in front of him.

He looked the soldier straight in the eyes. "What makes you think you love this girl, Russo?"

"Believe me sir when I say I do. I just can't bear being away from her. I just love her to pieces, captain."

The captain, the Company Commander of "C" Company, the United States Army 294th Engineer Combat Battalion and based in the grounds of Sherborne Castle, Dorset, nodded. "You say you love her? Does she love you?"

"Oh yes, captain, without a doubt."

"How long have you known her?"

Russo rubbed his hand across his mouth and screwed his eyes up, thinking hard. "It's almost a year now, sir."

"What about her family? What do they think about it all?"

Russo grinned. "They treat me like one of theirs already, captain. That family is the swellest family that I know."

"Do they know that you want to marry their daughter?"

Russo laughed. "You bet your bottom dollar, captain! Rosie, that's my intended, made me do it the English way. She said to me, "It's only right and proper that you ask my father's permission first." So, I had to ask him for his permission to marry his daughter."

The captain smiled, for he was aware of this quaint old English custom. It wouldn't cut any ice back in America, of course, but over here life was very different from that back home. It was a lot more formal and old fashioned and moved at a gentler pace. "And what did he say?"

Russo grinned. "He just stuck out his hand and asked me why I had taken so long to ask him."

The captain nodded. He looked down at the folder once again and read another line or two. He pointed at a paragraph and said, "Well, Russo. You seemed to have convinced the Padre of your intentions. He writes highly of you and is very supportive in his recommendation."

Russo's heart gave a leap. "Are you going to O.K. my request then sir?" he asked.

The captain nodded. He signed the bottom of the paper, dated it and said, "Your request to marry Miss Rose Welsh is hereby approved, Private Russo." He grinned broadly as he said in an authorative tone, "And you had better damn well make sure that I get a piece of that wedding cake, private!"

In the Royal Marine Inn at Yeovil there was a little discreet bar. There was an unwritten rule between the American visitors and the locals that only those couples with serious intentions used it. The much more bawdier and noisy single men and women used the main bar, or if they really fancied their chances, the lounge.

Russo sat at the round table with his fiancée Rose, sitting opposite him. They were holding hands and lovingly looking into each other's eyes.

Rosie could not contain herself any longer. "Well! What did the captain say?" She knew that her boyfriend had been to see his Company Commander to ask his permission to marry her. Her heart was all a flutter as she waited for an answer.

Russo's eyes took on a hint of sadness, and he slowly shook his head from side to side. Rosie's heart sank. "You know how hard it is to get permission to get married, Rosie. I saw him, and I asked him straight out for permission to marry you, and you know that I so much want to!"

Rosie's eyes became moist. She squeezed Russo's hands tightly. She wanted to cry but she knew she had to be brave. "Never mind, my love," she said in encouragement. "Let's leave it for a month or so and you can ask him again."

Russo let go of Rosie's hands. He picked up the glass of Bourbon that lay untouched on the table. He lifted it up before his eyes. "To us, Rosie," he said.

Rosie managed a brave smile and picking up her own glass returned the toast. "To us, my darling," she said. Both placed their glasses to their lips and Russo drank his down all at once. "Steady, my love," she mockingly admonished. "That stuff is hard to get around here. You need to make it last."

Russo grinned wickedly. "I'm celebrating," he said.

"Celebrating! What's there to celebrate about?"

The American soldier took his time. "It's not every day that your captain gives you permission to marry the woman you love!"

Rosie hands flew up to her cheeks, the importance of what had just been said suddenly striking home. Russo was grinning like a Cheshire Cat. Rosie laughed and jumped up, rushing around the small table to plonk herself firmly down on Russo's lap. She grabbed hold of both his ears and gave him a huge kiss. "You bastard!" she jubilantly cried.

Russo had told Rosie that he was going on exercise that next week, so after the weekend was over he would not be seeing her for a week or two. She understood that. It was war and these things happened.

The week or two dragged on, then another week or two. Still there had been no news of him. She had heard about an explosion in Sherborne that common gossip had said had been set off by two Nazi saboteurs in the US Army Hospital based in the grounds of Sherborne Castle, but that was all. It had caused no damage or casualties.

The month of May dragged slowly on by and she began to despair, crying herself to sleep most nights. What had happened to her Russo? She tried to find out but no-one knew anything. The American boys from Russo's company had stopped coming to the Royal Marine Inn, and no-one knew why.

Suddenly on the 6th June it was announced that the Allies had invaded France and she was ecstatic. Now she knew where he was. He was an American Combat Engineer and had gone to France. The invasion had been so secret that no-one knew that it had happened. It also explained why the boys of "C" Company 294th Engineer Combat Battalion had stopped using the pub. They had been whisked away somewhere to prepare for the invasion.

She waited at home every day for the postman to arrive. Soon she would hear from her beloved Russo and where he was. "God keep him safe!" she prayed fervently each night. But the months passed by, then the year. Then the war ended and the Americans went home.

She never married but became everyone's aunty. Rosie was always the bridesmaid, but never the bride. As time went on it became always the Godmother, but not the mother. She couldn't bear to live in Yeovil and to be reminded of how her American soldier lover had lied so glibly to her. She moved away to London and pursued a career as a Secretary, and a very good one she became too.

Every time she heard an American voice in the capital she would look to see if it was Russo, and if they were old enough she would ask them if they knew him in the vain hope that someone might someday said that they did. In 1986 she retired and finally made up her mind to return to Yeovil, her birthplace. No-one would remember her by now and no-one would remind her of her shame.

Then one day she read in the local newspaper that a group of servicemen that used to belong to "C" Company of the 294th Engineer Combat Battalion were visiting Sherborne and would be attending the local Remembrance Parade. She steeled herself to go and see them and resolved to speak to one of them. Finally, she would put her ghosts to rest and find out what had happened to her lover. What if Russo was there? What if he was amongst those returning veterans? What would she do?

In that event, she decided to do nothing. If he was there, he would probably be there with his wife and family. If he wasn't, she would innocently ask of an old family friend if anyone knew him.

That year the Remembrance Sunday fell on the 6th November. Her stomach was all butterflies as she got into her battered old Ford car and drove to Sherborne, finding somewhere to park with a little bit of difficulty. She had her black hat and gloves on and wore a large red poppy. Following the crowd, she walked down to the War Memorial.

Amongst the veterans on parade she saw the Stars and Stripes being proudly displayed, and one of the men was carrying a poppy wreath with the name of the 294th Engineer Combat Battalion emblazoned on it.

After the 2 minutes silence had elapsed the poppy wreaths were laid around the base of the war memorial. She watched as the American laid his. She had not seen Russo amongst the men and she shed a silent tear as she realised he had probably been killed on D-Day. Still, she just had to find out.

After the parade was over, everyone filed into the ancient abbey at Sherborne for the annual act of remembrance. Rose went inside and just managed to get a seat out of the kindness of a veteran who gave up his for her. Once the service was over she went outside again and stood on the road, waiting for the veterans and the American contingent to pass by.

After the march past had finished they all dispersed into a local car park. Gritting her teeth, she took her courage in her hands and approached the American man who had laid the wreath.

"Excuse me," she said.

The man turned to face her. "Yes ma'am," he drawled.

"I'm so sorry to bother you," she said timidly, "but when I heard that the 294th was coming back to Sherborne I just had to be here."

The tall American smiled. "Why, thank you ma'am," he said. "It's nice, but sad to be back and all at the same time," he replied.

"Yes, I can understand that." She just stood there, not quite knowing what to say next. The American looked her in the eyes and said, "Don't be afraid to ask me a question ma'am. I was the Officer Commanding "C" Company during the war."

Her heart leapt. "Then you must have known a family friend of ours. His name was Private Russo. We never did learn what happened to him. Was he killed on D-Day?"

The Captain looked at her with a quizzical look on his face. "And who might you be, ma'am, if you don't mind me asking?"

"Oh, you won't know me. My name is Rose, Rose Welsh." She reached out to the captain and they both shook hands.

"Oh, but I do know you, I think.   Weren't you the fiancée of Private Russo?"

She gasped as a roaring noise came to her ears. Her hand flew to her mouth. Through moist eyes she nodded. "Yes, I was," she said quietly.

The Captain stood studying her for a moment. He said kindly, "You don't know, do you? Not even after these years."

"Know what?"

The Captain contemplated his next words carefully. "Look, Rose. Do you mind if I call you Rose?"

"Of course not, captain."

"You must call me Steve."

"Thank you, Steve."

The Captain gently took Rose by the arm and said, "Follow me."

From the car park, they walked back to the War Memorial. At the front of the War Memorial the captain stopped and asked, "Have you not looked at this War Memorial before?"

"No," she replied. "After the war was over I moved to London to follow a career."

The Captain nodded his head and repeated himself. "You just don't know what happened, do you?"

Rose shook her head from side to side. "I only know that he said that he was going to marry me and that he would be away on exercise for a week or two." Her voice momentarily became bitter as she said, "I never saw or heard from him again."

The Captain sighed deeply. "It's time you learned the truth, Rose. The first thing I need to tell you is that Private Russo loved you deeply and was totally sincere in his wish to marry you."

Rose began to sniffle which turned into a dignified sort of cry. Try as she might, she could not stem the tears that rolled uncontrollably down her cheeks. A passer-by gave her a curious look. She felt as if the years had rolled off her shoulders. Now she knew for certain that Russo had loved her and had really wanted to marry her. He had not abandoned her after all!

"I need to tell you a story," said the captain. Looking around him he spotted a vacant bench. "Let's sit there," he said.

Sitting down Rose composed herself. She took a large floral handkerchief out of her black bag, and after wiping her eyes blew her nose, hard. The captain waited patiently for her to finish.

"Russo had seen me and asked my permission for you two to get married. You know, in those days you really had to prove that you were sincere in your intention. He was sincere alright." More tears began to roll from Rosie's eyes. The captain placed his hand on hers and asked gently, "Are you O.K."

She nodded, her eyes shining brightly. "Yes. Please tell me the rest, Steve, whatever it is."

The captain took a deep breath and said, "As always during the war, quite regularly we were on exercise. This one finished on the Thursday, the 20th March 1944. The task of the men had been to practise laying anti-tank mines in a perimeter around the US Army hospital in the grounds of Sherborne Castle, just up by the entrance gates. This they successfully did. After that the live mines were collected and stacked in a neat pile. A lorry parked in front of them. There must have been about 90 of the mines in all," he said.

Rose sniffed. "Go on, Steve," she encouraged.

The Captain nodded and cleared his throat, and this time it was his eyes that went moist. "We don't know exactly what happened. I was inside the hospital at the time saying goodbye to the colonel in charge of the place. There was a tremendous explosion and it threw us to the ground."

"There really were German saboteurs then," she added.

Steve shook his head. "No, that was a story we put out to cover what really happened."

"I need to know," Rose said, "warts and all. What happened next?"

Taking a deep breath, the captain closed his eyes for a moment, reliving that awful moment in time. "For some reason the truck rolled back onto our neatly stacked anti-tank mines. They all exploded at once, killing a lot of our men."

"Russo?"

"I'm sorry Rose," he said. Standing up he offered her his hand, which she took. He led her around the back of the War Memorial and there on the wall were two bronze plaques. The one on the right had the names of those of the 294th Battalion who lost their lives in Europe on active service post D-Day. The one on the left commemorated the names of the 29 US Army Engineers who were killed because of this explosion.

Her eyes ran down the three lists of names shown on the plaque. She was reading the far-right hand list on the plaque and had almost reached the end of it when she saw what she had dreaded. The fourth name from the last was all she needed to know. "Russo!" she cried as she fainted into the arms of the former American captain.

This tragic loss of American servicemen, and the second worst accident to the US Forces in Britain, occurred just before D-Day at Sherborne, Dorset, and it really did happen. The plaque itself carries the following inscription:

294th Engineer Combat Battalion

On March 20th, 1944, while completing their training for the invasion of Normandy, 29 members of "C" Company, 294th Engineer Company, were killed in an anti-tank mine explosion in Sherborne. This plaque is dedicated to their memory and reads:

Sgt Donald J. WALSH	PVT John P. DEEVY	PVT Leo A. LYON
T/5 Francis X. GALLAGHER	PVT John W. GADEK	PVT John J. McHUGH
T/5 Warren F. RAPP	PVT Robert GLADDEN Jnr	PVT Thomas S. NICOL
T/5Lawrence C. S. BARATTA	PVT George E. GUNDY	PVT Luclen P. PESSOZ

PFC Francis J. MURPHY

PFC Martin A. NORTON

PVT Charles W. BRINKOFSKI

PVT Robert M. BUCELLA

PVT Edward D. CHIARIERI

PVT Anthony CUTRONE

PVT Harry H. HANSCHKA

PVT Joseph B. HENNING

PVT Leonard B. KERR

PVT Stephen E. KOSIOROWSKI

PVT Roger E. KROEGER

PVT Conrad PROPP

PVT Robert L. READY

PVT Anthony T. RUSSO

PVT Andrew Ter WAARBEEK

PVT Fred C. TRACEY

PVT Joseph J. ZANELLI

Secret Army - 4th June, 1944.

Tom could sense that there was going to be trouble, he just knew it. The loud soldier had already consumed two pints of rough cider, and he just wasn't use to the sheer alcoholic strength of the famous local brew.

"You're a bloody coward, and that's all there is to it!" the big soldier sneered, baring his white teeth at the young barman. Tom shook his head and said in a tired, patient tone, "Look, I've told you once before. I have tried several times to join up but each time I turn up at the Recruiting Centre they turn me down at the medical. I've got something wrong with my liver."

The soldier jeered and pointing at him scoffed, "It's turned yellow, like the rest of you!" He glowered fiercely at the 19-year-old barman before taking another sip out of his almost empty pint of cider. Tom steeled himself, for he half expected a punch from the rowdy man to suddenly come flying his way. He would have loved to tell the soldier the truth, but he couldn't. Instead, on most nights he had to take the ragging he got from the servicemen who used the place because he was old enough to be a soldier but was not in uniform, not even in the Home Guard. He thought that if had been the first-world-war, someone would surely have given him a white feather by now.

The front door to the Pen Mill Hotel suddenly burst open, and to Tom's immense relief two British Military Policemen, accompanied by two white helmeted American Military Policemen, surged through the entrance. The American NCO put a whistle to his lips and blew it. The babbling and busy bar suddenly went very quiet.

"All service personnel are to immediately report back to their units!" he announced in a dramatic tone and in a distinctive Texas drawl. A derisive jeer rippled through the bar. The two American soldiers meaningfully drew long wooden batons from their leather belts.

"Come on now, this is an order from the highest possible level."

As if by magic, the crowded bar of the Pen Mill Hotel suddenly began to empty as the soldiers made their way out of the bar. The telephone rang and Tom answered it.

"Pen Mill Hotel," he said. He stood holding the telephone to his right ear. Nodding his head, he said, "Yes sir. I understand perfectly." Replacing the large black handset of the telephone back into its cradle he turned to see his antagonist finish his drink.

"What's up boy?" he said. "Your doctor ringing you to check on how you are?" The soldier laughed and slammed his empty pint pot down on the counter. "We real men have some work to do!" He laughed again as he turned away from the bar and walked out of the hotel, sauntering belligerently pass the Military Policemen as he did so as he threw them a challenging look.

Within minutes the place had been cleared of soldiers, leaving only twenty or so local Yeovil girls regretfully nursing their drinks. There were no men left and quite quickly they also decided to go, for there was no-one there to buy them another beverage. Tom glanced towards the landlord of the hotel, who just shrugged his shoulders.

"Big surprise exercise, I expect!" he explained. He took out his watch from his waistcoat pocket and closely examined the time. It was just coming up to nine o'clock and apart from the landlord and Tom, the place was empty. From being a crowded and noisy place the bar took on the aspect of an empty box and for the first-time Tom realised how loud the ticking clock on the far wall sounded.

He went out from behind the bar with the landlord and together they started to collect the empty glasses. Picking up a bucket and a shaving brush, Tom started to empty the full ashtrays that abounded around the bar. He used the shaving brush to carefully clean around each ashtray. The American soldiers who used the place often left long cigarette ends in the ashtrays, and Tom considered it a perk of the job. To him, these "dog-ends" as the Americans called them, were a useful bonus. He rarely had to purchase a packet of cigarettes for himself, although it took some time for him to get used to that strange "walnut" taste that the American tobacco reminded him of.

Pocketing a dozen large "dog-ends" he walked outside into the warm evening of that lovely day. It was the 4th June, 1944. He made his way around the four wooden tables that were outside in the garden and provided for the benefit of the customers. Tom emptied the ashtrays and was surprised by the amount of army trucks that seemed to be speeding up and down the road, some heading down to the nearby Pen Mill Station carrying all types of cargo. Down at the station a puffing train pulled away, steam hissing out from between its wheels. It made a "Chuff, Chuff" sound as it strained to pull the laden goods wagons that it had behind it.

By half past nine all the administrative chores of the Hotel had been finished. The glasses washed, the ash trays emptied, the bars wiped clean and the floor swept. Ernie Lewis, the landlord, took out his pocket watch once more. He frowned as he glanced at it, for not one customer had entered his establishment since the Military Policemen had emptied it.

"Lock up, Tom!" he suddenly announced. "We are not going to get any more business tonight."

Tom needed no second bidding, for because of the telephone call he was wondering how he was going to get the time off that he needed. Now the landlord had just given him that time.

The station at Pen Mill was now crowded with men moving about everywhere. Tents were hastily being pitched in the land behind the Pen Mill Hotel. A colonel had come into the Hotel with his staff and commandeered it, instructing the landlord that it would be a while before he could open again. Ernie, the landlord, grumbled about the loss of trade but he knew there was nothing he could do. The colonel had eyed him coldly and had said to him in a clipped accent, "You will be compensated for your loss of trade, landlord."

The landlord watched as an Army man walked past him carrying a large painted sign. It read, "Civil Defence Rendezvous Point No 24." Ernie resigned himself to the fact that there would not be any business over the next few days.

Tom had things to do and places to go. He thought about having a look at what was going on down at the station, but by now it was sealed off and the temporary road block was manned by Captain Browncie and his men of the Home Guard. It was dark by the time he got down to the river.

The 19-year-old timid barman's demeanour suddenly changed. He was now a confident young man, fully aware of what he was doing and where he was going. He waited for an opportune moment and crossed over the river bridge on the main A30 road that took him into the County of Dorset. Turning right he followed the River Yeo along and made his way into the thickly wooded area that ran all the way up to the top of Babylon Hill. Carefully he checked around him to make sure that he was not been watched. At a large Oak tree, he suddenly turned and started to ascend the steep hill, safe from any prying eyes that might have been looking in his direction.

Tom made his way up to a large Beech tree in the wood before he stopped and carefully listened. He stood still in the darkness for a while. Nearby, an owl hooted. Tom hooted in reply. He heard the safety catch of a weapon being set to safe.

A low voice called softly. "Summer?"

Tom smiled and gave the expected reply to the password. "Delight".

"Come forward and stand in that little moonlit area to your front."

Tom moved cautiously forward and placed himself firmly in the little ring of moonlight that penetrated the forest at this spot. "Can you see me?"

For a moment, there was silence. "Aye, Tom. I can see you. Come on up."

Tom walked forward slowly. Looking down at the base of a bush he knew well, he saw it being slowly parted by a hand. Ducking down on to his hands and knees he crawled through thick bushes and passed the sentry, his friend Paul.

Even though he knew that there was an entrance here he still found difficulty in locating it in the darkness. Pulling back some black Hessian cloth, he descended into a small hole. Wriggling through, he made his way along the concrete tunnel on all fours. After a yard or so the tunnel went off to the right and then after another two yards it turned sharply to the left, a defence against exploding grenades.

Pulling back some more black Hessian cloth he came out into a large cavern. It was lit by a solitary battery light. As he dropped out of the hole he noticed that a man was sitting on one of the three bunk beds and pointing a gun at him.

Tom grinned. "Evening, George. What's up?"

George put his pistol away. "Not sure yet, but we have been ordered on to active alert status."

"For how long?"

"I don't know. Till whatever the fuss is about is over I suppose.

The little Morse code set in the chamber suddenly began to tap out their call sign. The two men looked at each other in expectation as Tom grabbed the headphones, pencil and paper at the ready.

There were three men in this resistance cell, part of Britain's secret army. Their remit was to tell nobody who they were or what they did. In the event of Britain being invaded their mission was to remain behind enemy lines and sabotage as much of the invading German's equipment as they could, or to deny them the use of any British equipment left behind by the retreating British forces. They were the last ditch of defence in Britain and their life expectancy of this sabotage unit was three days.

Their main tasks were to blow up the three railway stations of Yeovil. Explosives had already been pre-planted at each site, and all they had to do was to detonate them. Tom was the one that had been trained by the Commando's. He would have to go ahead of his two colleagues if needed and quietly kill any sentries for them to carry out their acts of sabotage.

People chosen for this task would know the area intimately and usually had a good knowledge of the countryside. They would also have been taught how to survive in an invaded land. Each man had to sign the Official Secrets Act and was not allowed to tell anyone his real purpose, not even their wives or family. Tom was part of this one resistance cell. Unbeknown to Tom, there were another four such cells in the Yeovil area. He was also a member of the Home

Guard, although no-one knew that, and as such formed part of the GCHQ Special Reserve Battalion No 203 (Southern Counties).

Tom grinned to himself. He dearly wished he could have told that bullying soldier what he really did.

Royal Observer Corps- June, 1944.

Arthur Peabody was a member of Number 22 Group Headquarters, the Royal Observer Corps, and based at Yeovil. The unit was housed in a large underground bunker in a thickly forested area at Southwoods, just off Hendford Hill, and it had become a regular hive of activity in the early part of the war, but as the war progressed the manpower of the Royal Observer Corps had drastically been reduced to reflect this.

It was on the 3rd June 1944 that Arthur was sent for by the Observer Lieutenant Commander who was the officer commanding the group headquarters. Arthur was an experienced Chief Observer and his RAF styled uniform sported three chevrons that were surrounded by laurel leaves, which gave him the equivalent rank in the RAF to that of a sergeant. To distinguish the uniform as that of the Observer Corps he wore a Royal Observer shoulder flash on each shoulder, with the number 22 below it to show which group he belonged to. On each sleeve, he proudly displayed three Gold Spitfires and Stars that indicated the number of passes which he had achieved in the annual R.O.C. Master Test. Arthur knew his aircraft and was the best man in the group for quickly identifying aircraft, both enemy and friendly.

He knocked on the closed blue wooden door of his commanding officer with some apprehension. He did not know why he had been sent for. He had tried to recollect if he had done anything wrong or made any mistakes recently, but none came to mind. Arthur had grumbled that he would rather be out on an observation post than being in the headquarters, but that shouldn't be reason enough for the Observer Lieutenant Commander to want to see him.

"Come in!" boomed an authoritative voice from behind the closed door.

Arthur braced himself and entered the room. Behind the desk, smoking a Sherlock Holmes type pipe, sat the commander of the headquarters element of 22 Group. "Ah Arthur!" he said. He pointed towards a vacant seat with the stem of his pipe and said in an affable tone, "Take a seat old boy. I won't be long." In his other

130

hand the officer held a piece of A4 size paper that he was keenly studying. He sucked on his pipe and blew out a large cloud of smoke, some of it obscuring the Chief Observer for a moment. Arthur coughed, for he was one of the exceptions of the time who did not smoke.

The Lieutenant Commander waved the paper in his hand towards him in a vain attempt to move some of the smoke away from Arthur, for he knew that his Chief Observer did not smoke. "Sorry, old boy," he apologised.

"That's alright, sir."

The officer placed the paper face down on his desk and gazed sharply into Arthur's eyes. "I won't beat about the bush, Arthur. I have heard that you are not too happy about being shut up here in the bunker, leading the plotting team. Is this true?"

Arthur nodded and wondered who had told the commander about his grumbling. It could only have been the young observer officer who had recently been put in charge of the operational floor of the bunker. "Yes sir, I have expressed that opinion. I'm more of a 'hands on' man, really."

Lieutenant Commander Burke nodded. "Yes, you are," he agreed, "and a damned good one at that!" He thought for a moment and seemed to be formulating his words before he spoke again. "How would you like to be hands on again?"

Arthur's face brightened, for truly he was getting fed up with being shut up in the underground bunker whilst on duty. He would rather be up top and in the open air, plane spotting. "I would love to, sir," he said, barely keeping the excitement in his voice concealed.

Burke nodded his head again. "I thought so," he opined. There was a moments silence before he continued. "I have a job coming up that is right up your street. It is the most hands on job that you will ever have and it is classified as top secret."

"Top secret, sir?"

"Yes, very hush, hush and all that. Do you think you are up to it?"

Arthur eagerly nodded his head, a gleam of excitement showing in his eyes. "I am!" he exclaimed. "What have I got to do?"

131

Lieutenant Commander Burke shook his head and said, "I'm afraid that I can't tell you that, Arthur. What I want you to do is this. Go home now and pack enough things for a week. If anyone asks you any questions you are to say that as part of a group exercise you are being detached to the north of England, and leave it at that."

"That's no problem, sir. As you know I am a single man and don't really have any ties here."

"I know; and that is one of the many good reasons that you were chosen for this mission. I can tell you that it will be dangerous, and there is a chance that you might not come back."

"Might not come back?"

"No, you might not." The commander pushed a sheet of paper towards Arthur. "This is a Service Will Form, Arthur. Take it with you and fill it in. Be back here at 0600 hours tomorrow morning, ready to go with all your kit and equipment. I will give you more information then."

He took the offered piece of paper and folding it carefully in this pocket stood up from his chair. "I'll see you in the morning, sir," he said brightly.

On Sunday, 4th June, 1944, Arthur reported in to the Royal Observer Corps headquarters bunker at Southwoods in Yeovil. He was quite excited and didn't know what to expect. What he found when he got there was an RAF one ton Bedford vehicle and, to his surprise, two RAF policemen sitting expectantly astride their motorcycles. They eyed him intensely as he strolled past them.

Entering the bunker, he was directed to the briefing room where he found that he was the last man to have arrived, despite it being only a quarter to six in the morning. He nodded greetings towards a couple of Chief Observers that had already taken their seats. There was a look of expectation on their faces.

"Hello Tully, Rich!"

"Baint surprised to see you here, Arthur!" said Tully.

"What's up?"

"Buggered if I know," replied Richard. "I expect you had the same briefing as us?"

Their conversation was abruptly ended as the Lieutenant Commander suddenly entered the room and accompanied by the Observer Lieutenant. "Morning chaps!" he called brightly. The men rose to their feet.

A muffled and ragged chorus of "Morning sir," was returned by the men in the room.

Lieutenant Commander Burke sat down with his officer besides him. "Take a seat, lads," he said. "Everyone got their Will Forms? Good; pass them to Lieutenant Brand here."

Each man took out his Service Will Form and passed it forward. Lieutenant Brand scrutinised each one as he took it. He picked up one and passed it back to one of the Chief Observers. "You forgot to sign it," he said sternly. The Chief Observer quickly signed the document and returned it to the young officer.

The commander looked at his men, as if really seeing them for the first time. "Well chaps, we have one more thing to do before we can go any further. Hand them the forms, Brand," he ordered. Lieutenant Brand handed out a buff coloured form to each of the men present. The commander's voice took on a stern tone. "That is the Official Secrets Act. I want each of you men to read it, sign it and date it. Lieutenant Brand here will countersign it. Once you have signed it, I will be able to tell you what this is all about."

The men nodded their heads in understanding. Arthur didn't bother to read his form and promptly dated and signed it before returning it to the Lieutenant. After a few moments, all the forms had been completed and returned. Brand scrutinised them all before looking at his commanding officer and saying, "All in order, sir."

Burke said quietly, "Thank you Lieutenant Brand. You may leave us now." The young lieutenant left the room, quietly closing the door behind him. His departure was followed by seven pairs of curious eyes, for this really was Top Secret then.

Their commanding officer coughed to get the men's attention. "Now that you have all signed these forms I can now give you a general outline of what all of this is about. You may smoke if you wish." Several of the men took out packs of Woodbine cigarettes, the most popular brand of the day, and lit one up. A couple of them took out their notebooks. Burke saw this and shaking he head said, "Sorry, gentlemen. No note taking, if you please." The men looked curiously at each other.

Burke tamped the end of his pipe down and lit it. Taking a satisfying draw, he blew out the cloud of blue smoke to add to that of the room. It had a funny smell about it, Arthur reflected, a sort of scented smell. "We have been concerned now for some time about the number of friendly aircraft that have been shot down by our own side. The Royal Navy anti-aircraft gunners seem to be the worst culprits at this. Never could trust a sailor with a gun!" he quipped. The men laughed. The officer's face looked serious as he explained, "You are going to go aboard some D.E.M.S. to identify aircraft, either friend or foe."

Arthur put his hand up. "Excuse me, sir. What is a D.E.M.S?"

"I'm sorry; I'll try not to speak in acronyms. D.E.M.S. stands for Defensively Equipped Merchant Ships." Arthur nodded his head to accept this explanation and looking around he could see that some of the others were glad that he had asked the question. Burke continued. "This venture is known as Operation Seaborne. You will all be temporarily attached to the Royal Navy with the rank of Petty Officer/Aircraft Identifier." The officer pulled out one of the drawers from his desk and withdrew two large envelopes. He poured the contents from each onto the desk and in two separate piles. "Help yourself to two shoulder flashes and one arm band each," he said, pointing at the items with the stem of his pipe.

The men picked up the flashes and the armbands and then sat down again, eyeing them curiously. Each shoulder flash bore the words "Seaborne" and the armbands had the letters R.N. printed red in blue on them. "You will continue to wear your observer uniforms," he said, "but you will not remove the observer corps flashes. Sew the seaborne flashes beneath them, but remove your group identification numbers. Save them for later as you will need to put them back on again once this mission is over!" The men laughed. "Everyone got that?"

One of the men said, "Where are we going, sir?"

134

The lieutenant commander shook his head. "I can't tell you that either, I'm afraid." The men looked at each other. "When you leave here in that lorry you will be escorted by the two R.A.F. police motorcyclists. Only they know where you are going. Once you reach your destination, all will be revealed to you."

The lieutenant commander called out, "Lieutenant Brand!" The door to the office opened and the young officer stuck his head through the door. Before he could speak he was told, "Get the men onto the lorry."

"Yes sir!" Brand threw the door wide open. "Alright men, pick up your kit and follow me."

The men got up and picked up whatever they had with them. Some had little brown suitcases, others little canvas bags. In it was the kit that they needed. They had no webbing, for the Royal Observer Corps was an unarmed organisation. Talking cheerfully and speculating upon their destination the men left the underground bunker and got into the back of the truck. As they good humouredly jostled into the empty truck they gave their names to the R.A.F. police corporal who was going to lead them on their journey. He ticked off their names on a list as they did so.

Once everyone was in he said, "Listen you lot. All I know is the destination of where we are going. I shall just take you there and that'll be it as far as I am concerned."

"How long are we going to be?" someone shouted from the inside of the truck.

"We'll be as long as it takes. Sit back and enjoy the trip, for you will be going through some pleasant countryside and be seeing things that you never thought you would see. Does anyone need a piss before we start?

There was no reply so the Royal Air Force corporal turned about and sat astride his powerful motor cycle, kicking the engine into life. His companion did the same. The engine of the one ton lorry kicked over and it suddenly lurched forward downhill.

At the bottom of Southwoods the blue coloured vehicle with the R.A.F. roundel painted upon is side turned left and chugged its way up over Hendford Hill. At the Quicksilver Public House the lorry turned left again, following the main A.37 road.

They had not got very far before they encountered a road block at Whistle Bridge but they were hardly detained at all. A grim faced armed American soldier glanced briefly into the back of the vehicle before they were waved through.

Arthur sat on the tail of the lorry and had a good view as they drove along. The road was absolutely packed with men, stores and equipment. Everywhere one looked there were boxes and boxes of ammunition. He looked into the back of the truck at his companions and said, "I reckon that we are going to Weymouth!"

Historical Note: *The Royal Observer Corps (the Corps obtained the Royal part of their title in 1941) were officially a uniformed civilian volunteer organisation with affiliation to the R.A.F.*

The Seaborne Observers saw active service on D-Day (OPERATION NEPTUNE) on the D.E.M.S. They quickly and accurately identified enemy and friendly aircraft alike, keeping the number of blue on blue incidents (friendly fire) to a minimum. Twenty-Two Seaborne Observers survived the sinking of their ships. Two of their number were killed in action and several others were wounded.

This initiative was an unqualified success and in recognition of this fact His Majesty King George VI authorised those wearing the Seaborne flashes to retain them as a permanent feature of their uniform.

Ten Royal Observer Corps Seaborne Observers were awarded Mentions in Despatches. Each man was also awarded the France and Germany Campaign Star and the 1939-1945 War Medal. 795 members of the Royal Observer Corps took part in the D-Day landings and subsequent actions.

Camp 405 - August, 1944.

Private William Hirst, or 'War Horse' as he was commonly known to his friends and comrades, stood guard on the watchtower that overlooked the road leading to Barwick House, near Yeovil. He had a good view over the lake and the temporary huts that contained over 4,000 prisoners of war, most of them Italian. Next to him Private George Brown was sitting down, his back pressed against the rough planks that hid him from view of anyone approaching the sentry position.

George had a cigarette in his hand and occasionally put it to his lips to take a quick drag, carefully blowing the smoke away from him in small puffs so that the tell-tale sign of his smoking would not be spotted by anyone in authority. It was an offence to smoke on duty and he had been caught once before. That episode had cost him a whole week's wages.

He eyed 'War Horse' curiously for he was a rarity of the time, a man that did not smoke. In fact, as he warily eyed him, he noted that 'War Horse' never smiled. It would be hard for him to smile anyway, as the terrible scars that he bore on his face kept his mouth almost permanently agape. Regular as clockwork, 'War Horse' would drag his cuff across his open mouth to remove any spittle that might be gathering there.

'War Horse' nodded down towards the huts containing the German prisoners. They were kept separate from the Italians as there was no love lost between the two groups. "Best you get up here, George," he cautioned. "Looks like the duty sergeant is coming up to see us."

George quickly stubbed out his cigarette and placed the half-smoked portion of it in his pocket. Getting rapidly to his feet he picked up his .303 rifle and glanced down to the spot where he had been smoking. A piece of grey ash was settled there so hastily he rubbed his foot over it, erasing the evidence.

'War Horse' called down to the two men manning the barbed wire gate. "The duty sergeant is heading up towards us lads." One of the men waved to him, acknowledging that he had received the message.

The sergeant climbed the twenty feet up the ladder and entered the Observation Post. "Morning," he said. He stretched and stifled a yawn.

"Morning, sarge," replied George, eager to show his superior how efficient he was. "All quiet and nothing to report."

The sergeant nodded and looked out from the Observation Post towards the main gate. "Has there been any gate traffic?"

'War Horse' said, "The milk truck came through at 6 a.m. and the newspaper man at about 6.30 a.m. There's been nothing else since then, sergeant."

The sergeant looked at his watch. "It's 7.30 now," he observed. "There will be two working parties going out to the farms at 8 a.m. In the first there will be 60 Italians and two charabancs will arrive to collect them at a quarter to. They are off to Denmead Farm. No escorts will be going with them."

The two soldiers nodded. It was quite normal for the Italians not to have any escorts nowadays, particularly as the war in Europe was going so well in the Allies favour. It was a different matter for the Germans though.

The sergeant continued. "A working part of 10 Germans will be coming out at 8.30 under the command of a corporal and four men. They will be marched up to Yeovil Junction where they will be carrying out some work on the railway embankments. They are due to return at 5 p.m. and the Italians at 7 p.m." The sergeant scratched his head. "Watch those German buggers, men. They are true Nazis through and through. One of 'em upset the Officer Commanding yesterday by giving him a Nazi salute." The sergeant gave a wry grin. "He's making 'em cut a stinging nettle patch with no gloves and just sticks to beat the nettles down. That'll teach the buggers!"

The sergeant nodded to the two men as he left by way of the ladder. The two men exchanged glances. "Not much for us to do for the remainder of this duty," said George. "Roll on nine o'clock." They were due to be relieved at that time and so would have 2 hours

138

off before they came back for another 4-hour stint. George glanced down and saw the sergeant talking to the two men on the main gate, no doubt relaying to them the same information that they had been given.

There was a click as 'War Horse' took off the magazine of the Bren gun. Lovingly he checked the tension of the spring that pushed the bullets upward. Satisfied, he clipped it back into place on top of the gun. He fingered the safety catch off and then on again.

"You watch what you are doing there, 'War Horse.' We don't want an accidental discharge now, do we?"

'War Horse' gave what passed as a grin from his lopsided face. There was a hole where his teeth should have been on his left side of his mouth, and would have been if the shrapnel from the exploding German grenade hadn't hit him. "No fear of that," he replied. "Just wanted to be sure, that's all. Just in case them there bloody Nazis try something."

Private Brown grunted and shook his head. 'War Horse' might have seen plenty of active service but there was something not quite right with the man. He gave him a furtive glace and shuddered at the gleam in 'War Horses' eye.

The two charabancs arrived exactly on time and reversed from the narrow lane so that they were ready to drive out to Denmead Farm. At eight o'clock two groups of Italian prisoners, under the command of their officers and NCOs, came up the road in two separate groups. They did not march, but ambled along and chatted amiably amongst themselves in what was the beginning of a warm summer's day. As they reached the main gate they stopped as the two guards gave a head count. 'War Horse' watched them carefully, his Bren gun pointing lazily towards their general direction. A couple of the Italians gave him a friendly wave.

One of them called out, "Don'ta you worry Joe!" There is a film show tonight and we all wanna to see it!" The Italians laughed and the main gates were thrown open for them to get on the buses.

It was entirely different story with the Germans. They came marching up the road from their hut, lustily singing a German marching song. They were in perfect step and goose-stepping up the road.

'War Horse' snarled, a look of pure hatred on his disfigured face. "Steady there!" cautioned Private Brown, a worried tone to his voice.

Private Hirst sighted his Bren gun on the marching men as they came towards them, arrogantly singing their song. The British corporal led the way, with two escorting British soldiers marching on each side of the little column of Germans. The prisoners of war were goose-stepping two by two. 'War Horse' watched them intently.

The corporal brought the men to a halt beneath the watch tower as the two men on duty at the gate went to open it. It was then 'War Horse' saw it. "Bloody hell!" he shouted as he clicked the safety catch on his light machine gun to 'off'.

"Look out!" he shouted. "They aren't our men. They are Germans!"

As if to answer him the corporal lowered his rifle and shot one of the main gate sentries. 'War Horse' did not hesitate. He fired a short burst from his light machine gun, spinning the man around. Another of the escorting soldiers turned his weapon upwards towards the watch tower as the Germans made a break towards the gate. 'War Horse' coolly fired again, killing the man instantly. The other sentry was knocked to the ground by a rifle butt and 'War Horse' did not hesitate. He pulled the trigger again, spraying the men with bullets. Expertly he changed magazines, the gun hardly faltering in its staccato rhythm of death.

Private Brown stood stock still in shock and amazement, looking on in disbelief. "Bloody hell!" he cried as he nervously tried to bring his rifle to aim.

"Cover me!" ordered 'War Horse' as he exited the watch tower and slid expertly down the ladder, his weapon in his hand.

From the guardroom, armed men were tumbling out and rushed madly towards the main gate, uncertain of what was going on. By the time they had arrived it was all over. The sergeant ran gasping up to 'War Horse' and shouted, "What the bloody hell have you done?"

'War Horse' pointed at the dead and dying Germans with the barrel of his light machine gun. "They were attempting to escape I reckon," he opined.

"How do you know that?"

'War Horse' pointed the barrel of his still smoking Bren gun towards the body of the British corporal. "Look at that bugger, will you sergeant."

The sergeant looked at the dead soldier. "I can't see anything," he said, "except that you have killed the poor sod."

Private Hirst gave his lop sided grin. He walked over to the dead man and kicked the dead man's foot. "Ever seen a British corporal wearing Jack Boots?" he asked.

From the hut of the would-be escapees came a shout as a naked British soldier came staggering out of the building, blood streaming from a scalp wound.

"Bloody hell!" exclaimed the sergeant.

Historical note: Camp 405 really did exist at Barwick, although all the temporary buildings and barbed wire have long since disappeared. The camp was located at Grid Reference ST 5600 1446 and crop marks can still be seen where some of the huts stood. Over 400,000 prisoners of war were held in Britain during the Second World War.

It's Nearly Over Now - 18th April, 1945.

In 1945 the war in Europe was finally grinding towards its conclusion. The allies were closing in on Germany and the battle lines were edging closer to Berlin every day. For the first time, there was a spare capacity in manpower to allow soldiers to go home on compassionate leave. Gunner William Henry Sims of Yeovil was such a soldier who had cause to.

It was mid-May and Gwendoline Sims was trying to tidy up a little whilst the children were at school, but she was simply too exhausted to cope. She had been taken desperately ill with an almost fatal case of influenza, the same dreadful disease that had cruelly robbed her of her mother during the great flu epidemic of 1919. She was very frightened, not only for herself, but also for her two young children. Her doctor had explained that it would her take at least a good three months for her to fully recover. Tears welled up in her eyes and she barely managed to stifle a sob at the hopelessness of it all. She felt so alone.

Her doctor, being firmly ensconced as a bastion of the old school, had not told Gwendoline of what he intended to do for fear of upsetting her. Instead, he rather tersely wrote to the Commanding Officer of her husband's regiment, the 141st Field Regiment, Royal Artillery, explaining to him of the dire family predicament that one of his soldiers, Gunner Sims, now found itself in. In his considered opinion, it was vital that his wife had help from her husband as there was no other family support locally available to her. Gunner's Sims parents did live in Yeovil, he wrote, but currently both were also seriously suffering from influenza and they could offer little or no help and support. Having discharged his duty of care to his patient, the doctor then put her case to be back of his mind as he concentrated on his other sick patients.

Gwendoline sighed heavily as she went to make a cup of tea, her only real sustenance. Having put just enough water in the receptacle for just one cup, she barely managed to lift the heavy old fashioned iron kettle across to the fireplace to put it on to boil.

She looked across to the large alarm clock that stood on the bare wooden table. Its minute hand crept slowly forward and displayed the time as four minutes to eleven. Gwendoline opened the tea caddy and placed a small teaspoonful of tea into the teapot. She started to cry and her eyes wandered across to the kitchen cabinet where a large bottle of aspirin was kept. Miserably she thought for a moment or two of how simple it would be able to release herself from the wretched existence that she was now living. Then she thought of her children and her husband fighting in a far-off land. Angrily she cried out loud, "Snap out of it, you fool!"

Gwendoline flopped down into one of two the old-fashioned kitchen chairs and rested her elbows on its high arms. She really did feel awful today and would have gone back to bed if only she could have. The doctor had clearly forbidden that. "You must make the effort to move around, Mrs. Sims," he warned sternly. "I know that for two pins you would want to go and lie down, and that is only natural that after suffering such a severe bout of 'flu as you have that you would want to do so. But you mustn't! You will never recover if you do that."

The words of the doctor confirmed what she already knew. If only she could get some more help around the house, then things would be that much easier. The reality was that she could not afford to pay anyone to help her. The money to do so was simply just not there.

Steam came puffing out of the kettle and she walked slowly across to the glowing embers of the fire to remove it. She gave a little groan as she did so, placing the palm of her hand across her forehead, feeling slightly dizzy. Gwendoline stood quite still to allow the moment to pass and then managed to carefully make her way across to the table. She poured the boiled water over the tealeaves and, replacing the lid on the gaily coloured teapot, covered it with a hand knitted tea cosy that her mother-in-law had given to her as a birthday present just before the war had started. Even this relatively simple task was just too much for her. She flopped down in her comfortable high winged chair, and despite her best efforts, her eyes closed as she dozed off.

143

There was a sudden loud knock on the door and the soldier's wife stiffened. She was not expecting anyone. Gwendoline put her hand over her mouth and walked shakily towards the door. Through the frosted glass, she could just make out the hazy image of someone in a uniform. "Oh, my God!" she cried aloud, thinking that this was the duty officer of an army unit coming to deliver the fatal message that all soldiers wives feared in war.

She opened the door in worry and trepidation, expecting bad news. She screamed, but it was a scream of pure unbounded joy. There before her stood her husband, William. He grinned broadly at her. "Any chance of a cuppa?" he said, a huge smile etched upon his tanned face.

She threw her arms around him and cried in pure unadulterated joy.

Gunner William Henry Sims of the 141st Field Regiment, Royal Artillery, had been at home now for nearly eight days of the 12 days' compassionate leave that he had been given. "None too soon," he had thought to himself. Since he had returned from the fighting in Germany he had taken on all the housework and heavy jobs around the house, getting the garden dug and putting in some onions, potatoes and lettuces. His wife was recovering by leaps and bounds and the doctor was so pleased with her progress that he had told her to stop taking the tablets that she had been using on a regular basis. She had done this and not missed them at all.

It was early evening and they had finished their tea. "I'll do the dishes in a minute, love," he said.

Gwendoline smiled and said, "Oh no you don't, darling. I am up to doing that now, thanks to you."

William started to protest but she shook her head obstinately. "I'm determined to do them. You go on off down to the station to meet your mate."

"Are you sure?"

"Of course I'm sure!"

William buttoned up the Battle Dress blouse he was wearing, for although he was on leave he was still required to wear his uniform at all times. "I'll take him for a pint or two in the Pen Mill Hotel when he arrives. I should be back about 10 o'clock. Is that alright?"

She gave a merry chuckle. "Of course it is darling. Now be off with you!"

William gave his wife a kiss on her cheek and for the first time noticed that her cheeks had colour in them. He smiled. "Bye, my love," he said and walked out of the door.

It was early evening and William was standing on the road bridge overlooking Pen Mill station that carried all the traffic on the busy A.30 Exeter to London main road. He was idly watching the locomotives shunting around the yards and waiting for the train that was bringing his mate home on leave for a few days. He had recently received an additional two days of compassionate leave and knew that soon he would have to return to his unit, for his wife was steadily improving each day. He hadn't told her yet, but his purpose in meeting his pal was to hand him a letter to take back to his C.O., pleading for his leave to be extended by another four days. Whether he would get it or not remained to be seen, but in truth he was not all that hopeful. "Ah well," he thought. "No harm in trying."

The main Yeovil to Sherborne road was quiet at that time, although a little bit wet from an earlier rain storm. William heard a racing vehicle engine and out of idle curiosity glanced up the road towards Sherborne. He could just make out an army two-and-a-half-ton truck hurtling towards him and going at some speed. Just as it got to the railway bridge there came the sound of something distinctly metal snapping. The truck suddenly slid out of control sideways and headed towards the bridge parapet. He heard a woman scream and an alarmed voice shouting: "Look out, mate!" William put his hands out in a hopeless attempt to try and stop the mass of metal just before it hit him, but it was to no avail. He died in hospital without regaining consciousness some three hours later, a distraught wife and parents by his side.

145

LEST WE FORGET

Historical note: 885585 Gunner William Henry SIMS, Queens Own Dorset Yeomanry, 141st Field Regiment Royal Artillery, lost his life on the 23rd May 1945, aged 27. William was the son of William John and Agnes Sims of Yeovil. He was also the husband of Gwendoline Dora Sims of 25 Brunswick Street, Yeovil.

Back from the War - 3rd October, 1945.

The scarecrow of a soldier encased in a badly fitting uniform sat timidly in the corner of the train carriage, talking to no-one and painstakingly avoiding any conversation. He was painfully thin, his face a dirty jaundiced yellow colour. Occasionally he gave out a rasping cough that brought pain to his burning lungs.

The war in against Germany and her allies and the war against Japan had ended in the defeat of those countries. Now the prisoners were gradually coming home. Charlie Bright was one of them. He had drifted off to sleep and cried out aloud in a fearful shriek, frightening the young soldiers around him.

One of them roughly shook him awake. "Here mate! Wake up! You're screaming your bloody head off in here!" Charlie awoke with a start and defensively threw his arms above his head, awaiting a beating from a Japanese guard, but this was not to be.

"Jesus Christ!" someone in the carriage blasphemed. Charlie gave a little whimper and a tear ran down his cheek.

A Naval Nurse rose out of her seat in the far corner of the carriage and moved between the seats. She looked at the soldier next to Charlie. "Change seats, mate. I'll see to him." The soldier gratefully got to his feet and moved past her, taking his place in the seat that she had been sitting in. As he went past he was conscious of the smell of perfume that wafted around her slim body.

The nurse sat down and took Charlie's hand. She patted it and said in a soothing voice, "There, there. No-one's going to hurt you." She waited a moment or two, studying the deep sunken eyes in the pathetically thin face. Charlie's shaven head showed several deep scars. "Was it bad?" she asked sympathetically.

Charlie nodded. "I was a prisoner of the Japs for over three years," he admitted miserably. The other soldiers in the carriage eyed each other, for the stories of the Japanese atrocities that were heaped upon their prisoners were by now well known. The soldier's faces took on a look of understanding and compassion.

"How long have you been back, love?" the young nurse asked gently.

Charlie wiped his nose. "I landed yesterday at Southampton. Me and a load of others came back by a troop ship." He hesitated and then smiled before continuing. "I'm going home."

The girl nodded, giving a bright smile. The smile then came off her face as she asked, "Was it really as bad as they say?"

Charlie just nodded. Surviving in a Japanese prisoner of war camp needed a miracle. He had such a miracle in that he had been an excellent mechanic in the Royal Electrical and Mechanical Engineers. He could repair any engine. And that was his saving. The Japanese camp commander had been the equivalent of a British captain, a Rikugun Taii. His old staff car repeatedly broke down and it was up to Charlie to keep it going. The captain needed it to go regularly into a nearby town where he kept several geisha women, albeit that they had been local Burmese girls.

The captain had treated him better than most of his other prisoners, if you called getting beaten up regularly better than being beheaded. The thought of it made him shudder as he recalled the Japanese captain suddenly slashing out with his Sumari sword to neatly decapitate his friend who was standing next to him. His friend had not bowed quickly enough.

Tears came to his eyes and he put his hands up to his eyes to wipe them away. The nurse said nothing, just stroked his hand. After a minute or two Charlie had recovered sufficiently for her to speak to him. "Where are you going?"

Charlie sniffed. "Yeovil."

"Do you live there?"

Charlie nodded his head. "Yes. I was born and married there."

"You've a wife?"

Charlie nodded in acknowledgement. "Yes." He smiled. "We got married in 1941. About two months after we married I was sent with my regiment out to Singapore."

The nurse nodded. "Were you captured there?"

"No. Me and a couple of mates were ordered on board an old steamer that was going to Australia a couple of days before Singapore fell."

Charlie went silent. "What happened?"

148

He didn't like to talk about it, but somehow the gentle tone of the nurse was coaxing things out of him that he thought that he would never talk about. The whole carriage was silent and the soldiers were listening intently to what Charlie said. Somehow, he didn't mind, for some of them must have also experienced the horrors of war.

He shuddered as he recounted, "A Jap submarine got us. Slammed two torpedoes into the steamer and she went down like a stone."

"Is that when you were captured?"

Charlie gave a strangled laugh. "Captured? No. The Japs didn't give a hoot about us. They just buggered off."

The young nurse sat spellbound, for she had never heard such a tale as this. "Did you get into a lifeboat?"

"No, there were no lifeboats that survived." He faltered in his story and gulped some fresh air. The third soldier in the carriage on his seat side suddenly produced a small bottle of whisky and, screwing off the metal top, took a drink from it. He leaned forward and passed the bottle down to the nurse.

"Here," he offered. "Get him to have a swig of this!"

The nurse passed the bottle to Charlie and he gave it a doleful look. "I've not had a drink since before I was taken prisoner," he explained.

The soldier looked startled. "Then best you start again, mate. Take a swig!"

Charlie took a gently sip of the golden coloured liquid, the fieriness of it taking him by surprise. He gave a hard cough and his eyes watered. Charlie felt a wave of heat rising through his body and somehow, he felt better. He took another drink.

"How were you rescued?" she asked.

"I wasn't," he replied. "I drifted around for a day or two on a piece of wood and the tide took me ashore."

The nurse frowned. "Were you the only survivor?"

Charlie took another sip of the whisky. He closed his eyes and remembered the sight of the drowning women and children, slipping away from the wreckage one by one. The old steamer had been

149

taking the families of the officers to safety in Australia when it was sunk. Charlie and his mates were sent as their luggage handlers. He took another sip of whisky and his eyes misted. There were over two hundred women and children on that ship, he remembered. He was the only one to survive.

He shook his head. "I can't talk about it," he said. His body shook in revulsion as he recalled the thought of the black fins of the sharks that dragged struggling women and children down to an awful death. One had hit him but instead of biting him he took the young pregnant woman on the plank next to him. She had been lying flat on it but made the mistake of trailing her hand in the water. After she had gone, Charlie had taken her place on the plank. It was that action that had saved his life. Sated, the sharks had returned to the depths.

The nurse patted his hand again. "I understand love. If it's too painful to talk about, then don't." Charlie looked up to her with grateful eyes and nodded his head.

He thought for a moment and said, "I was sure that I was going to get away with it. I made it to shore and hoped I was safe." He shuddered as he recalled, "That's when the Jap patrol found me." His words tailed off as he remembered the brutal beating he had endured before being dragged off tied upside down on a bamboo pole and carried by two Coolies. His life as an animal had begun then, he thought.

The rattling steam train came to a halt. A soldier release the leather strap that held the carriage window open and it dropped down with a loud noise. He popped his head out of the window to look.

A loud voice on the train platform called, "Yeovil Junction! Yeovil Junction! Yer tiz me lovers! Change 'ere for Yeovil Town station and stations onward to Taunton!"

Charlie suddenly jumped up. "Christ!" he said aloud in realisation. "I'm home!"

The soldier at the window stood back to give Charlie room to reach up to the luggage rack above his head and remove a small

150

cardboard suitcase. It had all he possessed in the world. "Thank you," he said to the nurse.

She smiled at Charlie. "Welcome home, soldier," she replied and kissed him gently on the cheek.

Charlie nodded his thanks to the girl and stepped down onto the platform of Yeovil Junction, something he had not done for several years and something that he never thought that he would do again. The carriage door was slammed shut behind him. Along the platform several other soldiers with a smattering of civilians were making their way across the platform to another train that stood steaming and waiting. This was the train for Yeovil Town.

The train behind him whistled and he turned around to see the nurse waving at him. "Good luck, love!" she called merrily. Charlie waved back enthusiastically, for he felt suddenly felt much better.

"Yeovil Town next stop!" called a guard as he started walking along the platform, slamming open doors shut as he did so. Charlie hastily ran across the platform and jumped through an open doorway just as the guard closed the door. His heart beat wildly and it was then he realised that he still had the small bottle of whisky in his hand. Swiftly he drank down the remaining contents.

Five minutes later the train steamed into the town station at Yeovil. Someone in front of Charlie opened the door. He got out and looked expectantly up and down the platform, for he was hoping that his wife Sybil would be meeting him, but there was no-one waiting for him.

Charlie shrugged his emancipated shoulders, for it was not surprising that Syb didn't know that he was coming home today. The message obviously hadn't got through to her. He only had to walk about 500 yards and he would be home. With a thrill in his heart he started walking up the old familiar road, his heart racing as he passed the first of many of the streets pubs.

Jack Horton came out of the first pub in Park Street, his pipe puffing away in his mouth. Charlie waved. "Hello Jack! Still smoking that old pipe, I see!"

Jack Horton frowned. He did not know who the thin scarecrow figure of the soldier in front of him was. "Ow do "ee know I?" he asked.

Charlie grinned. "I'll tell thee tomorrow, Jack!" Already his heart felt light and all the problems of the world seemed to have dropped away from his shoulders.

Within a minute or so he was standing outside Number 162, its familiar two stone steps that were slightly worn in the middle leading up to a brown stained door. On it was an old fashioned black iron knocker. Charlie smiled as he remembered that it was his father-in-law who gave him that as a wedding gift. He took great pleasure in banging it hard on the wooden door.

Within seconds the door was pulled open by a little boy. Charlie frowned. "Who are you son?" he asked.

The frightened little boy took a step backwards and turned around. "Mummy!" he shouted.

Sybil appeared out of the kitchen, rubbing her hands on her apron and leaving a white smear of flour on it. She had obviously been making a cake or bread. She put her hands to her mouth. "Oh, my God!" she cried, turning deathly white at the sight of Charlie. She staggered back against the wall and threw her hands over her eyes. She screamed, "I thought you was dead!"

Charlie brushed past the boy and held Sybil in his arms. Sybil was crying. The little boy shook his mother's apron. "Mummy, mummy, please don't cry!" he pleaded.

The returning prisoner of war took a sudden step back as the realisation about the child suddenly hit him, hard. "Charlie," she sobbed. "Please don't be angry with me. I swear to God I was told you had been killed!"

"Who's the boy?" he snapped.

Sybil took a deep intake of breath. "If you'll have him, he'll be your son," she quietly whispered, a pleading look in her moist eyes. "He's never known a father."

152

Charlie stood looking down at the boy who smiled brightly at him, his white teeth shining through his coloured little face. "Hello daddy," he said.

Charlie didn't know what to say.

BATTY, Ron, 95
BRAND, Air Marshall, 46
CHURCHILL, Winston S., 106
ELFORD E.C.
Farmer, 102
LEST WE FORGET
ADAM, Duncan, Royal Engineers, 72
ANDREWS, Charles William Edward, Royal Army Service Corps, 72
BATSTONE, Florence Lilian Maud, civilian, 57
BATSTONE, Reginald, civilian, 57
BRIGHT, Winifred Annie, civilian, 57
BUGLER, Mary Jane, civilian, 57
COFFEY, Patrick, Royal Artillery, 64
FARWELL, Elsie, civilian, 95
FEARY, Alan Norman, Sergeant Pilot, R.A.F., 57

FORSEY, Leslie, civilian, 57
GAY, Norman Charles, civilian, 57
HAYWARD, Agnes May, civilian, 57
HORWOOD V.C., D.C.M., Alec George, Lieutenant, Queen's Royal Regiment (West Surrey), 42
HUSSEY, Albert Victor, Home Guard, 95
JOHNSON, Linda Christine, civilian, 57
LEAN, Geoffrey William, Pilot Officer (Navigator), 102
LILYMAN, Francis John, Royal Engineers, 72
LUMBER, Florence Gertrude, civilian, 57
McMAHON, Padraig De Valera, Sergeant (Air Guner), 102
MILES, Donald William, Sergeant (Air Bomber), 102

MITCHELL, Albert George, Royal Observer Corps, 95

MORRIS, Myra Joan, civilian, 57

NICHOLS, Alan George Holroyd, Sergeant (Pilot), 102

PALLISER, John Thompson, Royal Artillery, 64

PALMER, Alfred Aubrey, civilian, 57

PICKARD, Violet Ruby, civilian, 57

RENDELL, Cyril Henry, civilian, 57

ROSE, Frank William, civilian, 57

SIMS, William Henry, Queen's Own Dorset Yeomanry, 146

SMITH, Elizabeth Jane, civilian, 57

SMITH, Sydney George, Royal Artillery, 64

SPEIGHT, George, Royal Artillery, 64

TUCKER, Wendell Jesse, civilian, 57

WINGATE, George Frederick Richard, Royal Artillery, 65

WOOD, Francis Alan Dudley, Royal Artillery, 65

LEST WE FORGET - 294th Engineer Combat Battalion, U.S. Army

BARATTA, Lawrence C.S., T/5, 122

BRINKOSKI, Charles W., Private, 123

BUCELLA, Robert M., Private, 123

CHIARIERI, Edward D., Private, 123

CUTRONE, Anthony, Private, 123

DEEVY, John P., Private, 122

GADEK, John W., Private, 122

GALLAGHER, Francis X., T/5, 122

GLADDEN, Robert jnr., Private, 122

GUNDY, George E., Private, 122

HANSCHKA, Harry H., Private, 123

HENNING, Joseph B., Private, 123

KERRY, Leonard B., Private, 123

KOSIOROWSKI, Stephen E., Private, 123
KROEGER, Roger E., Private, 123
LYON, Leo A., Private, 122
McHUGH, John J., Private, 122
MURPHY, Francis J., P.F.C., 123
NICHOL, Thomas S, Private, 122
NORTON, Martin A., P.F.C., 123
PESSOZ, Luclen P., Private, 122
PROPP, Conrad, Private, 123
RAPP, Warren F., T/5, 122
READY, Robert L., Private, 123

RUSSO, Anthony T., Private, 123
TRACEY, Fred C., Private, 123
WAARBEEK, Andrew Ter, Private, 123
WALSH, Donald J. Sergeant., 122
ZANELLI, Joseph J. Private, 123
LILYMAN, 72
SERVED IN WW2
BARTHOLOMEW, H.R., Warrant Officer, Royal Navy, 102
DUKE, Frederick Alfred, B.E.M., Home Guard, 102
LEIGH-MORGAN, P.R., Sergeant (Air Gunner), 102
STALIN, Joseph, 107
WINGATE, Orde, 59

Printed in Great Britain
by Amazon

71106088R00095